Gold Rush

Union Army deserter Cody Black thinks Gold Hill is a safe place to hide out the war and make his fortune. But Cody finds prospecting to be a tough business and soon finds himself in debt to the local gold baron. Desperate for work, he is forced to become a deputy sheriff and now faces the very violence he fled the army to avoid. To make matters worse, a nefarious plot is afoot to tip the war in favor of the Confederates. Cody must battle Southern sympathizers, and his own doubts, to seek redemption and help save the Union in Gold Rush.

Gold Rush

Bill Grant

A Black Horse Western

ROBERT HALE

© Bill Grant 2018
First published in Great Britain 2018

ISBN 978-0-7198-2815-7

The Crowood Press
The Stable Block
Crowood Lane
Ramsbury
Marlborough
Wiltshire SN8 2HR

www.bhwesterns.com

Robert Hale is an imprint
of The Crowood Press

Typeset by
Derek Doyle & Associates, Shaw Heath
Printed and bound in Great Britain by
4Bind Ltd, Stevenage, SG1 2XT

CHAPTER 1

Cody Black looked up and down the main street of Gold Hill. Today was the start of the rest of his life. He took a step out of the general store where he had just sold his saddle and tack. The horse it had belonged to, an old army nag, was now the property of the livery. There was no way now he was going back. He patted his pocket on his new jeans, thankful that he had burned his army uniform before entering the town. The proprietor had raised an eyebrow when Cody walked in wearing only his long johns. Cody had waved it off by saying a bear had surprised him in the morning, in his camp, causing him to flee before he could dress. That seemed to satisfy the owner's curiosity.

Now, Cody wanted to put his past behind him. He didn't want the stares, or the hidden accusations that would come if he had walked into town wearing his Union colors. A deserter, a coward they would call him. But Cody couldn't handle the war. The sight of his friend, Tommy Gill, from the same Ohio countryside, going down, bayonet wound to the chest, was enough for him. He hoped Colorado Territory was the start of something new – rumors of gold in the hills had already brought a slew of prospectors. A good place to lie low, to hide out from the war, to forget.

Cody sighed as he walked down the main street, searching for a saloon. A tall, stiff drink was in order. That, and news of work. The livery hadn't offered much for his horse, nor had the general store owner for his tack. He had spent much of it on his new duds, so work was needed if he was to survive. Cody stopped into the first bar he came to, the Rusty Spur, and sidled up to the counter.

'Shot of whiskey please.'

'That'll be two bits,' said the stoic bartender.

Cody started, taken aback, 'Two bits? Mighty expensive whiskey here.'

'You new in town?'

'Just rode in.'

'That explains it, then. Gold Hill is aptly named. Miners come here, they get rich quick, wallets filled with money, and they spend a lot at the saloons. So our prices are higher than . . . where'd you come from?'

'Back East,' Cody stated without looking at the man.

'So our prices are higher than back East. So, two bits.'

Cody plunked the money down on the counter and downed the proffered shot. 'I'm looking for work. What's a fellow got to do to get a claim here?'

'The best stakes for gold mining have been taken. But miners are always selling their claims and buying new ones. If you need work one man to talk to is Gary Talbott. He owns Talbott's Mining, and hires green-horns to help mine gold. He's bought up a mess of claims, too. You know how to pan?'

'To be honest mister, I don't know much about mining gold.'

'Then I'd recommend talking to Talbott. His office is down the street, take a left by the bank and you can't miss it. He's got a big sign says "Talbott's Mining".'

'Much obliged, mister.'

The bartender nodded and said, 'Name's Ellis,' as Cody walked out.

Gary Talbott was younger than Cody anticipated. A little older than Cody, perhaps just north of thirty, with light blond hair and piercing blue eyes. He eyed Cody criti-cally as he sat in his highback chair.

'I can always use another miner. You know how to find gold?'

Cody shrugged.

'That's all right, we'll train you. Got a place to stay?'

'Nope.'

'You don't say much do you? All right then, you can stay at the mining camp. Talk to Shorty about getting a tent. Welcome aboard, Cody!'

Cody shook Talbott's proffered hand. As he was led outside Cody smiled: he hadn't been asked any ques-tions about his past. Perhaps he was safe here, in the Rocky Mountains, the first big mountain range he had come to after his mad dash from the Army of the Tennessee. The mountains offered solace and a chance to start over. Now it looked like it would pay off: he could hide out from bounty hunters until the end of the war, and even put gold in his pockets.

Talbott guided him out of his two-storey office building. 'The main camp is due north of the town. Here,' he handed Cody a letter, 'Give this to Shorty, he's the foreman, and he'll set you up. Good luck.'

Cody had no trouble finding the foreman. Shorty turned out to be a wizened old man, stooped by age, short like his name implied, with a long gray beard. He squinted, eyeing Cody. 'So, you say the boss wants you to work for us?'

'That's what I'm saying. It's all there in the letter.'

'Can't read.' Shorty crumpled up the letter in his hand and threw it on the ground.

'Then why did he. . . ?'

'Don't know, boss is forgetful sometimes. Anyway, you want a job, that's fine. You know anything about mining?'

'Nope.'

'I been mining since 1848, the California Gold Rush. That's fourteen years. I'll teach you how to pan. There ain't nothing to it, really. Boss has got what he calls a consortium, don't know what that word means, but basically you get the right to work here and a share of the profits.'

'Is it easy to find gold?'

'Easy? Depends on where you look. But what's really hard is keeping it in your pocket. Too many young fellers get a pocketful of gold, gold dust, nuggets, whatever, and then they spend it all on whiskey and women.

Then they're back out here looking for more.'

Cody sighed, 'Well, I'm willing to try.'

'Great, grab a pan and follow me.'

Cody took a pan out of a pile that Shorty had nodded to and then followed the old miner. The camp was a sprawling mess of tents and lean-tos, surrounding a creek bed. Men, and they were exclusively men, sat around on logs, while some had waded into the creek to pan for gold. A group of man were using a sluice to run water from the creek, others were breaking rocks in a nearby quarry.

'Now, the mechanics of this are real simple. You just take that pan there, and dip it into the water – make sure you get the sand and silt from the bottom. Bring it out, and sift through all the sand. When you see something that glitters, that's gold. Set it aside and continue panning until the day's end. You can also break rocks, that's harder work, but maybe you'll find more gold.'

'It sounds tedious.'

'What?'

'Boring, it sounds boring,' Cody said with another sigh.

'That it is friend, that it is, but by sundown you'll have a lump of gold to put in your pocket.'

Cody nodded, this is what he was here for. This, and to escape the war.

'You got a roll?' Shorty asked.

'What?'

'A bedroll? A tent? Anything to sleep in?'

'No, there's nothing. I sold everything when I came here.'

'All right, I'll set you up while you work. Get you a tent and three squares a day. You can pay for it up front or it will come out of your earnings.'

Cody nodded, 'Got it, Shorty, much obliged.'

Shorty shuffled off, and left Cody alone to pan for gold, no questions asked, just the way he wanted.

CHAPTER 2

For the next several days Cody continued his panning. On his second day he found gold nuggets, a small amount, in his pan. He was so excited, he told Shorty right away. The old miner gave a snort. 'Keep panning, young one, there's more gold out there.'

The third day brought a little more gold, but the fourth day he came up empty. Same on the fifth and sixth day. In the camp Cody kept to himself: he had a small tent, a cup for coffee, and a tin to eat beans in. The other miners were a miserly lot, they weren't talkative, which suited Cody just fine.

One night, after a week at the mining camp, Cody was sitting alone on a rock, eating his tin of beans. Another miner was eyeing him, making Cody nervous. At length the man stood up and wandered over to Cody.

'Looks like a mighty fine place to sit and eat some beans. Mind if I join you?'

Cody shifted uncomfortably, 'It's a free country.'

'Much obliged. My name's Hank. Hank Grimes.'

11

'Cody. Cody Black.' He shook Hank's proffered hand.

'What brings ya to Gold Hill? Wait, lemme guess, the gold.'

'Yeah, I want to make money. Also, I kind of like the mountains,' said Cody, before he took another mouthful of beans.

'Lots of fellas come here. Most lose their money and drift away. I been here six months and haven't made my fortune yet. You look like a sticker though, maybe you'll stick around.'

'I hope so, at least for a few years.'

'Not going back East, uh, fight in the war?'

Cody gave Hank a hard look, his hand flexing unconsciously into a fist. He sighed, 'Not my war.'

'Don't blame ya. I'm from Texas, but I couldn't care one whit about fighting. Lot of fellas here are the same, but some aren't. Be careful what you say and who you say it to.'

'I'll keep that in mind.'

'How's your panning coming?' Hank asked, leaning over.

Cody pulled away, then sighed. 'I had luck on the second day, but since then I've hit a dry spell.'

'Yeah, payment is coming due for the tent and tools. Ole Talbott's got a good scam going. He doesn't get his hands dirty, and makes money off our sweat. Still, better than trying to defend your own claim. Claim jumpers will shoot you quicker than you can blink. Well, good talking to ya Cody, don't be a stranger.'

Cody watched in silence as the loquacious Texan

12

stood up and walked away to join some of the other miners. Two months ago he would have been preparing to kill Texans like Hank, but here in Gold Hill all that was in the past.

Cody frowned as Shorty counted out the gold nuggets. 'You're still short. The boss ain't gonna like that.'

'Is that why you're called Shorty, always telling the miners they're short?'

Shorty gave a dry chuckle. 'You're a funny one, ain't ya? You're short, ya gotta pay up. This will cover the tent for the week, but not the food.'

'It's only beans.'

'Ya still gotta pay for 'em.'

Cody looked away, not saying anything, as Shorty took all the gold nuggets.

'See ya next week,' the foreman said. 'Better have more gold or you might get kicked out.'

Cody punched the air in frustration. All of his hard work gone. The deserter stood there for a while, trying to compose himself. He had no choice but to continue panning for gold until he had paid Talbott. Cody picked up his pan and walked back to the creek.

'Trouble?' Hank asked as he squatted in the cold water.

'Yeah, Shorty took all my gold and said I still owed.'

Hank nodded, 'Yup, that sounds like Shorty. He does whatever the boss tells him. Talbott found him drunk in a saloon, his pockets empty. At least that's the talk around camp. Boss cleaned him up and made him a foreman. He knows gold, and he follows orders, only requirements I guess.'

'How do you and the others make any money here?'

'Heh, it takes a while to find your bearings. Everyone here has had trouble one time or another, but eventually they figure out right where the gold is. It takes patience, lots of it. 'Course there are fellas that never figure it out. They don't last too long. I hope you're not one of them. Have you tried breaking rocks?'

Cody wiped his brow. 'That's back-breaking work. I'd rather pan.'

'You're telling me. Wish someone would invent something that would make it easier to smash those big boulders into tiny pieces.'

'Ha, that'll be the day. Well, back to it, I guess.'

'Good luck, I'll see ya at chow time.'

Cody bent to his task, more determined than ever to find gold. But by evening he had only found a few specks of dust. Looking around, he saw other nearby miners had panned more than him, nuggets, in some cases quite big. Dang, he thought, maybe I don't know how to do it. It seemed easy when he first came here. From talk he had heard gold was running in rivers down the mountain. Apparent to everyone but him.

Cody sat down on his favorite rock, eating yet another helping of beans when Hank came by. 'Any luck?' the Texan asked as he plopped himself down next to Cody.

'Only a little bit of dust today. I'll tell ya Hank, if I don't get a break soon I'm gonna be flat broke. I need to do something to keep Talbott and Shorty off my back.'

Hank gave a low whistle. 'Don't know what to tell ya . . . hold on a second.' Hank stood up, looking at something brewing across the camp. Cody followed his line of sight and saw two men squaring off, arguing.

'Looks like a fight, come on Cody.'

Cody followed Hank, and they pushed their way through the gathering crowd of men. 'I told ya, that there is my gold. I found it fair and square.'

'Not likely Stan, it's mine, I put it there.' The second speaker brandished a knife while Stan made for his own belt. The knife wielder lunged at Stan, causing the man to jump back. Cody and Hank had made their way to the front, Hank yelling 'It's Stan and Eaton fighting.' Cody nodded, not needing the commentary.

Watching the fight reminded Cody of his time in the army. Every few days there would be a scuffle of some sort, usually over cards. But here, this was different. A knife had been pulled, meaning a struggle for life and death. These miners were deadly serious about their gold. Cody watched in fascination as Eaton swirled his knife, large enough to kill a bear, through the air. Stan's eyes grew wide every time the knife got close. Suddenly, he dashed around Eaton, coming straight for Cody and Hank, Eaton hot on his heels. As he passed Stan tossed a small pouch right at Cody. Eaton eyeing it, ignored Stan and ran right to Cody. 'Got my gold do ya? In cahoots! I'll slice you just as easy.' Cody had almost no time to react as the armed man bore down on him. Dropping the pouch, Cody reflexively brought his fists up. He grabbed Eaton's knife hand, stopping the blade inches form his face. With the other, he slammed his fist into the bigger man's nose. Blood splayed out, and the man's head snapped back.

Blinking away tears Eaton tried to attack again, but Cody held his right hand fast, twisting it until the knife, involuntarily released, hit the ground. Cody punched Eaton again and then dragged him to the ground. The angry miner struggled to get up, but Cody positioned his body on top, pinning him. Eaton's exertions became less and less pronounced as he gasped for breath. Soon he gave up the struggle altogether. Strong hands lifted Cody from the ground and dusted him off.

'How d'you manage that?' asked Hank, while slapping him on the back.

'I don't know, it happened so fast I just reacted.'

'Lucky me. Many thanks partner.' It was Stan, his hand out. Cody shook it and said, 'I didn't have much choice after you threw the gold at me.'

Stan picked up the pouch, 'Yeah, well, I had to do something.'

'My gold, give it to me,' Eaton, now standing, roared as several miners restrained him. The foreman took his time getting to the scene.

'What's all the fuss here?' asked Shorty.

'Eaton tried to knife me for my gold,' said Stan between breaths. 'Thanks to Cody though I escaped.'

'That's my gold. He durn stole it from me.'

'We'll get this sorted out, but Eaton you drew a weapon. That's not allowed in the camp. Take him to the stocks, we'll have the sheriff come. You say Cody helped you?' Shorty looked at Cody, puzzlement in his eyes.

Cody, his hands still shaking, nodded.

'Hot damned, Eaton's no small fry and when armed and angry he's about as unstoppable a force as we got on this here mountain. How's the gold hunting comin' son?'

'Not well,' Cody confessed.

Shorty scratched his long beard. 'Umm, boss is gonna want something from ya, and ya ain't good at finding gold, but y'are one hell of a fighter.'

'I was just. . . .'

'Nonsense, we'll find something for ya, if'n ya can't mine any gold.' Shorty waved Cody silent. Soon the camp's attention was focused on Eaton as he was dragged away, and Cody, for a moment, was forgotten.

'I bet Shorty is figuring on getting you a job with the sheriff. He's been looking for some new deputies,' said Hank.

'What happened to the old ones?' Hank gave Cody a knowing look, but said nothing.

'Talbott and the sheriff are real close. The boss needs law and order around to protect his claims. If you can't cut it as a miner, maybe Talbott will put in a good word for you. Land sakes, I never seen a punch like that. Ole Eaton isn't one to go down easy, and you dropped him like a sack.'

Cody only shook his head. 'I reacted, that's all. I had no time to think.' This was the last thing Cody needed. He had deserted battle to flee from violence and sense-less killing, now he was right back in the thick of it. Dang that Stan, he thought.

'Don't be modest. Looks like you're gonna stick

17

around here after all, partner.' Hank slapped him hard on the back, then followed the crowd of prospectors to find out what would become of Eaton. Cody, left alone, his hands still shaking, relived the moment he hit Eaton. He had no choice: it was either defend himself or be gutted. Perhaps tomorrow this would all blow over, forgotten by all, and he would find more gold.

CHAPTER 3

Tomorrow came, and the fight was not forgotten: it was still the talk of the camp. Cody's luck didn't turn either, he still couldn't find enough gold to pay off his debt to Talbott. It looked bleak for Cody as the second week drew to a close. He had to face Shorty with less gold than the week before. Cody remained stiff while Shorty counted the gold.

'You're still short,' the old miner said with a grin. Cody was convinced he got a secret thrill every time he said someone was short.

'So what does that mean?' Cody asked, his eyes darting nervously.

'That means you gotta talk to the boss. You been here two weeks and you ain't made enough to even cover your chow. You're gonna get deeper and deeper in debt unless ya do something quick. Talk to Talbott, he might have other work for ya.' Shorty gave him a knowing wink.

Cody sighed and nodded. He knew Shorty was right, he hadn't made the fortune he had expected. But he was afraid to talk to the boss, concerned that he'd turn him into a hired gun – exactly the reason he'd abandoned the army to avoid. Cody shuffled off, resigned to his fate, while Shorty dealt with other miners.

Talbott was sitting in his office when Cody walked in. He was writing in a ledger. At Cody's approach he looked up. With a half smile he said: 'Mr Black, what can I do for you?'

Cody swallowed – he always had trouble around authority figures: 'Mr Talbott, Shorty said to talk to you about . . . about my work.'

'Ah, yes. It seems . . .' he opened his desk drawer and pulled out another ledger '. . . that you've fallen behind in your payments. Now Mr Black, I am a forgiving man, and a patient one, but I am also running a business. If I continue to let you pan for gold and you continue not to have success you will end up owing me more money. So, any suggestions on how to resolve this crisis?' He drummed his fingers on the desk.

'Well, I don't rightly know. If you give me more time, I'm sure I can find. . . .'

'Time is a luxury we don't have any more. I can smell a bad investment a mile away, and you, son, are a bad investment.' He paused and stood up, walking toward his office window. 'My foreman says you're a good fighter, not afraid to mix it up. You saved the life of a fellow prospector. Those are qualities I can admire. There's a lot of money out here and a man needs muscle to protect his claims. I know the sheriff personally, he's looking for new deputies. If you consider hiring on, and work for a spell, I'll wipe your debt to me clean.'

'If not?' asked Cody.

'If not, well . . . we have ways to deal with debtors out here. I hope you'll say yes.'

'How much do I owe you?'

'Sixty-five dollars.'

Cody closed his eyes tight and exhaled a deep breath. It was the one thing he didn't want to do. He couldn't make that amount of money panning for gold. He was next to useless as a miner. Talbott was giving him an ultimatum he couldn't refuse. 'All right, I'll do it,' he said.

'Excellent, why don't you move your gear out of our camp and report to the sheriff. His name is Joe Corrigan – I'll tell him your coming.'

'Thanks,' Cody muttered as he left the office. His idyllic stay was turning into a nightmare out here in Colorado Territory.

Cody wanted to leave the camp in a hurry. He didn't have many belongings, only the clothes he had bought from the general and a few odds and ends. He checked his poke: he had only four dollars to his name. Talbott was robbing him blind. He wondered how many others had ended up broke and indebted to the stakes owner. Cody sighed and said goodbye to Shorty and Hank.

'It's a good thing you'll still be around,' said Hank as Cody began walking back toward Gold Hill. 'I'll have someone to talk to when I go into town.'

'Remember, I'll be a deputy or some such thing, I can't play favorites. Don't be gettin' into any trouble and expect me to get you out.'

'Don't I know it. I'll be seeing ya, pardner.' And with that, Cody left the mining camp behind.

The sheriff's office was little more than a hole in the wall: one room, plus three adjacent and empty jail cells. Joe Corrigan was middle-aged, with thinning hair, but a thick, bushy mustache adorning his face. He was chomping on a cigar when Cody entered.

'About time you showed up. Talbott sent a runner over two hours ago, said you'd be here any minute. Never mind that, you're here now. Name?'

'Cody Black.'

'You have any previous law enforcement experience?'

Cody shook his head.

'Any experience with a gun?'

Cody nodded.

The sheriff stared at him, taking his measure, then said 'All right, that's good enough. I lost the last two deputies I had. One to the drink, and the other one plumb left. Said he couldn't handle the mountain life. I hope you'll stick around son.'

'I aim to.'

'A man of few words, eh? Good, you'll fit right in. I'll get you a badge. You have iron?'

'I sold it when I got here.'

'None too bright, are ya? All right, you can have one of my spares. I got a Colt Dragoon my former deputy used to wear. Try it out.' He reached into his desk and pulled out the .44, tossing it to Cody. Cody felt it in his hands. It had a good balance to it. 'Here's the holster. Your job is to patrol the town, keep the fighting to a minimum, lock up disorderly drunks, and above all protect Talbott's gold. He's the major player in town – without him Gold Hill would collapse. If you ain't got nowhere to bunk, there's a small room right above the jailhouse, just a bed mostly. Your weekly wages are two dollars, no charge for the room.'

'And my debt to Talbott?' asked Cody.

'Heh, so that's how Talbott got you to come. You'll have to talk to him about it, but if he says you're clean, then you're clean. Let me get you a badge and you can start today.' The sheriff stepped into the back and returned with a star. 'By the powers invested in me by the Territorial government I hereby deputize you Deputy Cody Black.' He pinned the star on Cody's lapel. 'You're legal now. Strap on your gun and get to work.' Joe sat back down at his desk and resumed chomping on his cigar. In a slow, smooth motion Cody buckled his holster and slid the Dragoon into it, wondering now just what in tarnation he had done.

CHAPTER 4

Freshly deputized, Cody Black wandered around Gold Hill. He needed to familiarize himself with the town if he was going to be of any success in this new job. His outlook was starting to improve. As long as he worked, Talbot wouldn't collect on his debt to the mining consortium, he had steady pay, and he didn't have to eat beans three times a day. He didn't know how long he needed to work as a deputy to keep Talbott from collecting, but he figured it would be for a few months.

The only thing he worried about was drawing iron. That wasn't something he was looking forward to. As he strolled along on his first day of the job he would touch the butt of his Dragoon. It was an Army revolver, one reserved for officers, so he had never had a chance to fire one. He hoped the sight of it alone was enough to discourage lawbreakers.

His reverie was broken by shouts of 'Sheriff!' and a man running up to him, waving his arms. 'Sheriff!' the red-faced man said.

'I ain't the sheriff, I'm his deputy.'

24

'Close enough. We need your help at the Tin Cup. A fight's breaking out!'

Cody inwardly groaned. The Tin Cup was one of the many saloons that had sprung up in the wake of the first gold rush. It was a place haunted by doves, card sharks and lowlifes all waiting to strip a newly enriched prospector of his hard-earned gold.

'All right, I'm coming.' Cody had no choice but to follow the man. If he turned tail he'd be hunted down and be swinging from a tree before daybreak. 'Who's fighting?'

'Some of the local boys are accusing a man of cheating at cards. Come quick, or there'll be blood spilt for sure!'

Cody trotted along beside the flustered man, who told him he was the owner of the Tin Cup. When they arrived at the saloon Cody swung open the batwings and surveyed the scene. It was a stand-off. Cody recognized several miners from the camp huddled on one side of the room, facing a lone man wearing a black, wide-brimmed fedora popular among gamblers. The fingers of his right hand were dancing on the handle of a Remington Navy, holstered on his side.

'You're a lousy cheat. Pull up your sleeves, let's see that ace!' A prospector was yelling and pointing at the gambler.

'Gentlemen, gentlemen, it's not my fault you lot are poor card players. I won fair and square.' His eyes darted around the room, his body tense, but his demeanor calm. Cody guessed he was a professional and would gun these drunken prospectors before he could blink.

Cody cleared his throat and stepped through the doors saying, 'Everyone calm down now.' His voice came out smaller than he expected, and everyone ignored him. He tried again, aware the owner's eyes were on him. 'Everyone, listen up.' Again, no result.

'Hey, I got the law here. Now just quit it and listen.' The owner's voice carried through the room. Cody looked sheepishly at the owner, but the burly man only nodded, his eyes expectant. Cody took a deep breath and waded into the fray. 'All right, what's going on here.'

'This man cheated at cards. Now he won't give us our money back,' said the miner who had yelled earlier.

'I am not a cheat. You can hardly blame me for the way these fellas play cards.'

'What happened?' Cody asked. A chorus of voices started jabbering at once. The deputy held up his hands. 'Enough, one at a time. Just tell me what happened.'

'He cheated.'

'How do you know?'

'He kept winning. Ten hands in a row. No one is that lucky.'

The gambler shrugged. Cody had to act fast, all eyes were on him, and the prospectors, a group of five, were riled. One tried to grab for the gambler who danced out of his reach. 'Simmer down, I'll handle this. How much did he win?'

'He took all our weekly earnings.'

'What's your name?' Cody asked the gambler.

'My name's Hewitt. Lionel Hewitt.'

'Well, Mr Hewitt, you didn't cheat these fellas did you?'

'I maintain my innocence.'

'Do you have any evidence this man cheated?' Cody asked the group of miners.

'Check his sleeves, he's got an ace up there or I'm a broken-down mule.'

Cody made a motion for Hewitt to roll up his sleeves. The gambler removed his hand from his Remington and proceeded to do just that. He turned his hands back and forth in the air showing no cards.

'Anything else, deputy,' Hewitt asked in a bored tone.

'He's hiding it somewhere. I saw that ace!' The first miner was becoming belligerent now, pushing forward, he was almost on the gambler. Hewitt reached for his iron and Cody knew this was about to get violent.

'Stop!' He held up his hand. 'That's enough. I'm the law and there's no evidence this man cheated. He won fair and square, you're all just drunk. That's my finding.' The miners kept pushing forward, now jostling Cody. He tapped the butt of his Dragoon. 'Don't make me pull this out. Now git, and come back when you sober up.'

The sight of Cody's gun brought the miners up short. With much grumbling, they shuffled for the door. 'Watch your back, dandy. Someone might gun for ya,' one miner said as a parting shot. When they were gone Cody wiped the sweat from his brow, and let out a breath he didn't realize he was holding.

'My thanks, deputy.'

'What for, you're innocent, right?'

'Not everyone sees it that way. I'm a professional gambler, and my . . . ah . . . fellow players don't understand how good I am at my profession.'

'And that piece of cold iron?'

Lionel tapped his Remington. 'Tool of my trade. In case there are disagreements about how good at cards I am, like today. Fortunately I didn't need to use it.'

'I saved your bacon once, but don't make a habit out of riling up these prospectors. They can get real mean when they're liquored up, and there's a hell of a lot more of them than you. If I was you I'd lose a few hands every now and then. It might keep your head out of a noose.'

'How long have you been a deputy?' the gambler asked, his eyes narrowed.

'This is my first day,' Cody said, his face flush.

'Well, why don't you worry about sheriffing, and I'll worry about gambling.' He tipped the brim of his hat and headed to the bar.

Cody didn't realize how sweaty his palms were until after he stepped outside the saloon. He got lucky that he didn't have to drag iron. His bluff on the miners had worked, but he knew he couldn't rely on bluffing forever – one day there might be a hombre who wanted to trade slugs with him. He needed a stiff drink, but didn't want to booze while on duty. Still, he couldn't help himself from walking into another saloon, which doubled as a cathouse. There weren't many women in town, but those there were frequented the saloons. He strode straight to the bar, signalling the bartender for a shot.

'Hey, that's that lawdog what sided with the card shark.'

Cody flinched. Right next to him at the bar stood the loudmouth miner from the Tin Cup, right behind him were his buddies. Just his luck, he thought.

'Come here to steal from us again?' the miner pressed.

'I didn't steal from you. You have no evidence Hewitt cheated. He's a professional gambler, he's gonna beat you more than you will him.'

The man scoffed but kept his mouth closed as Cody tapped his Dragoon. The deputy downed his shot, plunked a coin on the bar, and left without a word. He could feel the miners' eyes on him, full of hate. Cody started to think being a lawman was a lot harder than he thought. A bottle crashed as the sun faded and he heard whoops in the distance. Yes, this job would be a challenge for him. But as long as he didn't have to draw his gun ... Cody wanted to delay that possibility for eternity.

The next morning Cody nursed a headache. He had stopped at three other saloons and was offered a shot of whiskey at each, and at the last one the bar tender had poured him four, on the house. Cody needed that many just to calm his nerves. A pounding at his door made his head hurt even more. 'Get up Deputy Black, we've got trouble!' Sheriff Corrigan poked his head into the room. 'Rough night last night?'

'Don't remind me,' Cody said, pulling on his boots.

The sheriff waited until he was ready, then led him outside. 'Trouble, deputy. There's a new card shark in town and he's made plenty of enemies.'

Cody thought of Hewitt.

'There's a big mob of miners in the center of town, they got him tied to a horse. There might be a lynching.'

Cody saw what the sheriff meant when he stepped outside. Not far from the jail was a group of around fifty men all surrounding a man, dressed in black, with his hands tied, mounted on a claybank. It was Hewitt. The sheriff pushed his way through the crowd, Cody on his heels, until they reached the horse.

'Now everyone calm down. What's going on here?'

'Sheriff,' it was the loudmouthed miner from the night before. 'We've determined this man is a cheat at cards. Last night your deputy prevented us from getting our stolen money back. He sided with this gambler. He continued to win by cheating. Now we want our money back or we're gonna string him up.'

'Is this true?' Corrigan whirled on Cody.

'They couldn't provide any evidence the gambler cheated. He's a professional, they're not, so I let him go with a warning.'

Joe looked at him, his mouth agape, his eyes wide. 'Son, you've got a lot to learn about being a lawman. All right, Mister gambler, where d'you hide the winnings?'

'Hewitt.'

'What?'

'My name is Lionel Hewitt, and I believe you should

listen to your deputy. He is wise beyond his years.'

'That's enough out of you. The money, now!'

Hewitt looked around, and then defeated, sighed. 'I hid it. In my room at the Tin Cup, there's a loose floorboard under my bed. There you will find these fine gentlemen's money. Now, may I be released?'

'Just hold it there. Why don't you fellas go check.' Before the sheriff could finish speaking, at least twenty miners were off to the saloon. Less than an hour later, the men returned, one carrying a large sack. 'It looks like it's all here, Sheriff.'

'Divvy it up. Everyone satisfied?'

The prospectors, after a bit of squabbling over the money, finally agreed they were satisfied.

'Fantastic, now may I be released?' Hewitt asked.

The sheriff eyed the gambler. 'By rights I should have you strung up. Instead I'm gonna run you out of town. If you ever show your damnable ugly face in Gold Hill again, I'll see you swing from the highest tree. Is that his horse?' One of the miners nodded. 'Now git,' he slapped the rump of the claybank hard, and the horse bucked once and galloped away. Hewitt struggled to keep himself from falling. Cody watched him go, his face becoming red. Corrigan looked at him and with a gesture said, 'Come with me.'

His head hanging low to avoid the jeers and looks of the assembled prospectors, Cody followed like a beaten dog. When they were back in his office the sheriff turned on Cody, his eyes cold. He fought for self-control as he started his tirade: 'Look here son, I know you're new to lawman work but you gotta use your

31

noggin. Don't be such an idiot. A professional gambler is always gonna cheat, and it's far easier to run one gambler out of Gold Hill than deal with twenty or thirty riled-up locals. Next time think about it before you go and make a decision like letting a gambler off the hook. I don't want to have to clean up your messes. If you slip up again, I'll take your badge. Got that?'

Cody managed to mumble, 'Yes sir.'

'Good, now go do more patrolling.'

Cody left, not wanting to waste his breath arguing with his boss. He still didn't think he was wrong, but let it go. No harm was done and he still hadn't been forced to use his gun.

CHAPTER 5

Lionel Hewitt steadied his claybank as they cleared the town. His wrists chafed under his bonds; they were tied tight. He didn't waste time trying to untie the knots. Instead he spurred his horse on gently, using his knees to guide the claybank until they reached a rocky ledge. A lone horseman stood there, unmoving, silhouetted against the sun. The man wore a gray duster. His wide-brimmed hat, also gray, was pulled low over his eyes. A thin mustache adorned his otherwise clean shaven face. He didn't even flinch when the gambler rode up next to him.

'Saw you coming a mile away, Lionel. Quite amusing seeing you try to ride with no hands.'

'I'm glad I could entertain you. Why didn't you come and help?'

'More fun watching.' The horseman moved his mount closer and with a flick of his wrist grabbed an Arkansas toothpick from his boot. He deftly cut through Lionel's bonds. The card sharp began massaging his wrists.

'So what'd you learn?'

'I learned, Jeffrey, that despite my appearance to you bound as I was, the town of Gold Hill is ripe for the plucking. What passes for law and order there is just one over-the-hill sheriff and a greenhorn deputy.'

'Are either of them trigger happy?'

'I don't know about the sheriff, but the deputy is gun shy.'

'How did you surmise that?'

'Oh, I see it in his eyes. He's afraid to draw. Sure, he makes a lot of noise about drawing, but he's all talk. No, we don't have anything to fear from him.'

'Is he young?'

'Very much so – perhaps he's a deserter.'

'Which side, I wonder?'

'Wonder not,' Hewitt gave a smile, 'since I think it hardly matters.'

'I see your point. We wouldn't want someone who ran from his duty to the Confederacy. And if he's a Yankee, he ain't worth spit.'

'My sentiments exactly.'

'Who ran you out of town?'

'A group of disgruntled miners, and lousy card players, who couldn't handle my winning.'

'Your cheating, you mean. Don't get careless, Lionel. I don't want you fouling this up. Any trouble from them?' Jeffrey asked.

'I don't think so. Miners can't shoot to begin with, and when they're in their cups, as they often are . . .' he let the comment rest and Jeffrey only nodded.

'They have the gold, though?'

'More than enough for our needs.'

34

'Good,' Jeffrey nodded his head. 'We're camped not too far from here. We got a plan to deal with the lawmen?'

'The sheriff, yes. The greenhorn, no need at all to worry about him. He'll flee at the first sound of gunfire. I have him marked.' Jeffrey smiled, turned his horse around and Hewitt followed him.

For the rest of the week Cody attended to his duties as deputy, and soon settled into a routine. He'd wake up, eat his modest breakfast of grits, eggs and bacon, and patrol the streets. The action didn't start until the afternoon or early evening when the miners would head for the bars. Then, Cody would have to break up drunken fistfights over cards or land stakes, or even arguments over politics and the war. Occasionally a knife would be involved, but so far no guns. Cody was grateful for that. For the first few days Eaton had been locked in a jail cell. Cody tried to avoid him, and ignore his curses and threats. He told the sheriff about their past and Joe agreed to have Eaton moved to Golden to stand trial for attempted murder. Once Eaton was gone, Cody relaxed a little more.

Rumours had spread in the town that Cody was a quick draw and a dead shot, making the prospectors and other denizens of the saloons reluctant to draw their iron. The deputy didn't know who started the rumor, but every now and then he would see his friend Hank Grimes in a saloon. The Texan would give him a nod and a wink. If it was Hank, as he suspected, Cody was quietly relieved. He didn't have to prove himself.

He only hoped it wouldn't bite him in the end if some gunslinger wanted to challenge him.

Four days after Cody became deputy, he was sitting in the small office that doubled as the jail when Joe burst in the door. 'Oh, good Cody, you're here. I need you to take charge today.'

'What for?'

'I got a message here that was left at a saloon for me. It says I'm needed to settle a dispute over land between a couple of prospectors, about half a day's ride from here.'

'Why didn't they come into town?'

'Probably didn't want to lose their respective claims. Another prospector left the message. It shouldn't take more than a day to sort it out, I'll be back tomorrow.'

'That sort of thing happen a lot?'

'It's not unheard of. I reckon I don't have much to fear with you holding the fort. Am I right, deputy?'

'Yes sir, I'll be just fine sir.'

The sheriff gave him a sharp look, then said, 'I'll be seeing you, Cody. Don't let me down.' Cody nodded grimly as Joe left. Now he was alone. He hoped nothing bad would happen while Sheriff Corrigan was gone.

Cody settled in to his routine, patrolling the street and checking the saloons. He stopped into the Tin Cup and saw Hank gabbing with fellow prospectors at the bar. Cody was about to leave when Hank saw him, waving him over. 'Hello Deputy, or is it Sheriff now? Some fellas saw Sheriff Corrigan hightailing it for the mountains.'

'He has a dispute to settle, so I'm in charge until he

gets back, tomorrow.'

'Well, why don't you have a drink, seeing as your boss is gone.' Hank ordered a shot of whiskey. Cody shook his head.

'Ah, come on, just one. It won't kill ya,' said Hank. He was egged on by his fellows.

'All right, just one shot.' Cody tossed back the whiskey. 'I've got to go, I'm still working here.'

'One for the road.' Cody took the shot and two more after that. He left the bar, but at the next saloon he stopped in, he was offered another couple of shots by someone who said he was Hank's friend. Now his head was spinning. He wasn't much of a drinker, and the whiskey was strong, like rotgut. He couldn't focus his eyes as the sun set. Cody decided to call it a night and sleep it off. Next time, he thought, I'll have to refuse any and all drinks. The tenderfoot drinker crashed on his bunk without taking his boots off.

The next day Cody woke up, his head pounding. He was happy that the sheriff would be back today. He poured a cup of coffee and waited by the desk. It was already after noon, Joe should be back in a few hours, Cody thought. But Joe didn't come back that afternoon. It was after dark and the sheriff hadn't arrived, so Cody reluctantly went on his patrol. He stopped in the Gold Hill Saloon, where the letter had been left for him.

'Hey, Fred,' he said to the bartender as he came in. 'Have you had any word from Joe?'

'Nope, can't say I have.'

'How long does it usually take to get back from there?'

The old man scratched his salt and pepper beard. 'Clear Creek? Not too long. Of course, it might take him a while to resolve the dispute. Or he could have been ambushed by Cheyenne, or bushwhacked, or a grizz. . . .'

'Thank you Fred, I'll assume it'll take him some time to settle the land dispute.'

Fred shrugged, 'Suit yourself.'

Cody was a little worried as he left the saloon. Any of those scenarios that Fred had suggested could have waylaid the sheriff. He hoped Joe was just delayed and would return in short order. He decided to forget his worries in some boon company – as long as he could refrain from drinking, that is. Walking into the Tin Cup, he found Hank perched on the same bar stool from yesterday. 'Have you even moved?'

'Of course I have, Cody. I went back to the camp last night and made it back here just a few minutes ago. Right, Mack?'

'Whatever you say, Hank,' said the bartender.

'Have a seat. Where's Joe? I thought he'd be back by now.'

Cody shrugged his shoulders. 'Don't know – hope he comes back soon.'

'You should have another drink while you wait.'

'It's mighty tempting Hank, but I don't want a repeat of last night.'

Hank gave a low chuckle: 'Can't hold your liquor, eh. Good thing you're a quick shot, otherwise you might be good for nothing – prospecting, drinking, cards, ya can't do any of that.'

Cody gave him a weak smile. 'Yeah, I'm not good for nothing.'

'Sheriff! We need the sheriff! Quick!' A prospector, shouting, burst into the saloon, the batwings flying behind him.

'I guess he means you,' Hank looked at Cody.

The deputy sighed and got to his feet. 'Sheriff's not here. What can I do to help?' The prospector scowled at first, then saw Cody's star. 'Come on, I'll show ya.' Cody followed the prospector, he was middle-aged with an unkempt beard, standard among the citizens of Gold Hill. When they got outside Cody saw the problem. Two men were staring at each other down in the middle of the street: the beginnings of a draw fight. Cody wasn't sure what the rules were for gunfights in Gold Hill. Joe hadn't told him anything, just said to patrol the town, look out for trouble and break up bar fights. Now he had a real gunfight to deal with. He steeled himself for what he might have to do, wiping the sweat from his palms. 'How'd this happen?'

The prospector shrugged. 'They were drinking, then they got to arguing over something, now it's led to this. You gonna do anything?'

Cody stepped in between the two men. A crowd was now gathering around them, making Cody all the more nervous. He put his arms out, 'Now just hold on here. What do you fellers think you're doing?'

The gunslinger to Cody's left twirled his thin mustache. 'Fight's fair, we don't need no lawdog.'

39

'He's right,' his opponent said. 'Let us settle this. Get out of the way.' Cody hesitated, unsure. He glanced at the prospector who just shrugged his shoulder. 'You're the law. Just wanted to let you know what was going on.'

'You'll have to wait till the sheriff gets back. So both of you stand down.' Cody's hand hovered near his gun belt. The gunmen ignored him. 'Do you hear me? There won't be any shooting today.' No one moved. Cody took a step forward, intending to stop the closest gunman. No sooner had he done so, then crack, crack. Two shots, and just like that, it was over. The man with the thin mustache lay dead; his killer checking his Smith & Wesson. Cody stared at the dead body in the road, his heart frozen in his throat. It was like Shiloh all over again.

'Better get the undertaker for that body,' the prospector said as he passed by the deputy.

'Right, I'll do that,' Cody managed to say, his throat dry. The crowd was now staring at Cody, but he couldn't take his eyes off the body, and couldn't move.

'Ever seen a dead body before, lawman?'

Cody didn't answer, he didn't know who said it. Now a murmur started in the crowd. One word stood out above the others: 'Coward.'

CHAPTER 6

Lionel stood on a ridge looking over Gold Hill, Jeffrey beside him. 'It looks like this town is bereft of any law and order.'

'Make sure it stays that way. When Julius gets back, we'll hit the shipment from Talbott. There's enough gold in them hills to turn the tide of this war.'

'As you say,' Lionel muttered, too loudly.

Jeffrey turned on him, frowning. 'Don't need you going soft on me now, Hewitt. Your job is to take care of any lawmen that might be down there. You say there's just one deputy now, and a yellowbelly at that. Julius is coming tomorrow, that shipment is coming in on pack mule from the camp straight to Gold Hill. We got to get it before it's secured. No foul-ups.' He pointed his finger in Lionel's chest for emphasis. Normally Lionel would have killed a man for doing that, but Jeffrey Cranster was a hard man. His partner Julius Tucker was even worse. Lionel had sympathies for the Confederacy, but these men took it to the extreme. As long as he was paid, he kept reminding himself.

'All right,' he said. 'No foul-ups.' Jeffrey seemed satisfied and walked back to his horse. Lionel stayed where he was for a while, watching the town.

Cody got the body of the dead gunslinger to the undertaker with some help from Hank. It wasn't until after they had left the body, paying for his funeral expenses with what they found in his pockets, that Hank broached the topic Cody was dreading.

'So what was that all about. I mean, with you staring at the body and all, after you told 'em not to shoot.'

Cody kept walking, not wanting to talk about it, his eyes forward, his cheeks becoming flush. But Hank persisted, 'Why didn't you move?'

They turned the corner into an alley, and when Cody thought no one was looking he wheeled on Hank. 'Because I. . .I don't know, maybe I was scared, that's why. Were you in the war? Death and violence, they ain't easy things to look at.'

For once the loquacious Texan was silent.

Cody took a breath and continued. 'I came here to ride out the war, just prospecting for gold. I didn't ask to become a deputy. And I hope I'm never forced to drag iron, because I'm not sure I can do it. Why d'you start that rumor about me being fast on the draw? Now I look foolish.' He kicked a rock in frustration.

'You are fast, Cody. Your reflexes are, anyway. I saw what you did to Eaton. He's bigger than you and you took him down. True, I ain't ever seen you draw, so don't know how fast you are with a gun. But if you can shoot straight you can take on all comers.'

42

'That's the problem, ain't it Hank. I don't know if I can do it. I get all nervous just thinking about using a gun.'

Hank gave a smirk. 'You didn't have much problem taking on Eaton.'

'That was different. He had a knife, not a gun, and I reacted.'

'Right, you didn't think about it. So don't think about using your gun, just do it when you need it.'

'It's not that easy, Hank. I got to manage until the sheriff gets back, then I'm hightailing it out of here; my debt to Talbott be damned.'

'If he comes back you mean. Where'd he go?'

Cody shrugged, 'Into the mountains somewhere. Something about a claim jumper. He'll be back soon.'

'You hope.'

'He will, you'll see. I need to get back to the jail.'

'Yeah, I better mosey on back myself. The camp's abuzz. Gold shipment's coming down in two days. All of Talbott's gold we've helped him acquire is headed for Denver.'

'I didn't know about this.'

'Yup, happens every few months. Talbott always uses an armed escort. Sheriff knew – oh, but he's gone. See ya Cody.'

Now Cody started to worry as he walked, his gait plodding. What if Corrigan had been waylaid somewhere? Things were going from bad to worse for the deputy. Lost in thought he almost bumped into the man in a tan duster standing near the jailhouse. Cody looked up and recognized him as one of Talbott's men.

'Talbott wants to see the sheriff,' he said without pre-amble.

'Sheriff's gone.'

'Who's in charge?'

'I am.'

The hired hand jerked his thumb. 'All right, then Talbott wants to see you.'

Yes, things were definitely going worse for Cody.

'I want your men on either side of the wagon, and some outriders.'

'Why so many?'

'It's a precaution, Cody. We're moving a lot of gold and I want none of it stolen. It makes a tempting target. So your men will ensure the wagon gets to Denver. You have men ready, don't you?'

'What does the sheriff normally do?'

'Beats the hell out of me. I tell him I'm moving gold, and he shows up with about ten or fifteen men in a posse, and they escort the gold to Denver. It saves me money.'

'I thought you had men.'

'I only have five men working for me in this town, and that includes Shorty and the driver. The sheriff provides security. When's he getting back, anyway?'

'I . . . I don't know.'

'Well, the shipment can't wait. The day after tomorrow meet the wagon at noon in the town center with your men. Do whatever you have to do to rally them. Don't make me regret doing that favor for you.' Talbott turned his back, and Cody figured the conversation was over. Once outside the deputy walked aimlessly, his mind distracted by events. He was becoming over-whelmed. Then newly determined, Cody made a decision. He needed to find out what had happened to Sheriff Corrigan. At least then he'd know what he should do next. He had two days before Talbott's wagon was ready.

Cody didn't waste any time. He saddled up and rode off in the rough direction he thought Joe had gone. But he wasn't the best tracker, and Joe had been gone for two days now. Cody guessed he would have headed into the mountains. It shouldn't be hard to pick up his tracks, he thought.

He thought wrong. Cody hadn't gone more than a few miles into the mountain country when he knew he was lost. This wasn't like back home in Ohio, where the land was flat. Here the mountains twisted and turned and they all looked the same. It was mid-afternoon when he left Gold Hill, now the sun was setting and he was ill prepared to spend the night in the Colorado wilds. Too impulsive, he'd thought finding the sheriff would be easy.

Cody stopped his gelding. It was a borrowed horse, one of two allotted to the sheriff. He patted its neck absently as he thought about what to do. He could go on, trying in a futile effort to find the sheriff. Or he could go back to town and try to salvage his reputation before everyone thought him a coward. Then he heard a rustling in the brush and saw a grizzly cub wander right in front of him, and stop. He froze, and the horse began to shy away. Where there was a cub, there would be his ma. Sure enough, a female grizz came barreling through, and stood right next to her baby.

Cody froze as he watched the mama bear rise on its hind legs and give a roar. The gelding's body shook under him, and Cody backed it further away. The big grizzly didn't back down and stared down Cody as he put distance between them. Cody saw the bear didn't follow, but stood her ground until he was over a hundred yards away. Then, unhurried, she ushered her offspring along the trail. The bear had no fear of man when defending her cub, and a sudden realization began to dawn on Cody: he was afraid and running.

The townsfolk and Talbott would think for sure he'd run away. Shirked his duty to guard the gold wagon. That settled it, he must go back to town. His instincts, his cowardly instincts he reminded himself, led him to find the sheriff – let him handle everything. But the sheriff isn't coming back, he was strung up or dead somewhere. Cody was in charge and he had to accept that. If the grizzly bear is unafraid of man and his fearsome weapons, then he shouldn't be either. Cody wheeled his gelding around, hoping to backtrack as much as he possibly could in the fading twilight. He only hoped he wasn't too late to escort his former boss's gold.

CHAPTER 7

Lionel woke with a start. The cacophony of thundering hoofs accompanying the riders was enough to wake the dead, or at least the whole camp. He knew before he even stood up that Julius Tucker had returned. Soon the camp came alive with a flurry of activity. Dawn was cracking over the horizon, and the word came to break camp. Lionel stuffed his bedroll on to his horse and checked his Navy Remington. Looking around he caught Jeffrey's eye and wandered over to him. 'What news?' he said.

'It's time to go. The last shipment is ready in Gold Hill. Julius is back. It's all set.'

Then Lionel noticed a string of pack mules being led into the makeshift camp. He looked curiously at Jeffrey. 'Julius made some stops along the way.' He had a sly smile on his face. Then Lionel understood – the gold, or part of it. 'We hauling by mule all the way down to Mexico?'

'Nope, we'll transfer the gold to the wagon.'

'What wagon?'

'The one we're gettin' at Gold Hill. Enough questions, mount up. You've got to scout ahead, make sure we take the town by surprise.'

Lionel was eager to go. Soon this whole messy business would be behind him, and he'd be a very rich man. He rode off, but not before he passed Julius, attempting to make eye contact. The brawny leader ignored him, instead directing his men moving the mule train, a gleam in his eye. Lionel didn't care much if Julius's plan worked and saved the Confederacy from defeat. He only cared about being paid, and his employers looked ready to fulfill their end of the bargain. As he rode past Julius he counted ten men who rode with him. That was five less than what he left with. There were fifteen men in the camp, not including himself and Jeffrey. Twenty-five men plus Julius, Jeffrey and himself. Lionel nodded – still enough to haul the gold down to Mexico, where the French troops were waiting. Waiting to enter the war and help the Confederacy.

Cody stopped briefly in the night to sleep. He had made progress before it became completely dark. His own trail was still fresh and he remembered some of the landmarks, but now he'd have to wait until morning. If he got back to town by noon, he'd have just one more day to find enough men to escort the gold wagon to Denver. He woke before the dawn, wary of bears, coyotes and Cheyenne. He'd only brought his Colt with him, not thinking he might need something with more firepower, like a Henry. So far he had been lucky. As he rode, his attention focused on the path, looking for tracks – but then his horse stopped. Skittish, it started to move around, its head moving from side to side. Cody wasn't used to handling it, but tried to bring it under control.

Then he saw what was causing it to be so jumpy: a bear rumbling toward them. One look told him it was a black bear, not the big grizzly he had seen before. Dang bears are everywhere, he thought. Scared, he fired one shot in the air, causing the bear to veer off into a thick grove of aspens. Cody didn't bother to wait, but pulled the gelding in the opposite direction, putting some distance between them. Damn, he thought, it might be a while before I can get to Gold Hill.

It wasn't until late in the afternoon when Cody stumbled into town. He'd been lucky: a traveling prospector had heard his shot, and, curious, had gone to find out what was happening. He had pointed Cody in the right direction – but it had still taken him a few hours to get there. Now he had less than a day. What's more he remembered the conversation he had with the prospector. 'You a deputy? I'd be careful if I were you. I just came from Clear Creek down south. Word was they had a major bank robbery. Big shoot-out, sheriff killed, all their gold cleared out. What's more, a train of pack mules carrying gold from the mountain camps went missing. Some group of bandits is running around the territory stealing all the gold. A young tenderfoot like you is liable to get dead shooting at random bears like that. Especially if these gold thieves see that tin star on your shirt. Deputy, ha, can't even find your way around. I'll show you where Gold Hill is.'

Cody had taken the man's ribbing in good stride, but he was troubled by his news. If the prospector was right, and Cody had no reason to believe he wasn't, then there were one or more groups of outlaws out there robbing gold. He wondered if Gold Hill was next – then he thought, what if the sheriff had run afoul of them? It would make sense.

Cody rode up to the jail and unsaddled his gelding. His stomach growled and he needed coffee. There was a small kitchen in the back of Joe's office where Cody found some eggs and coffee beans. He ate his eggs quickly, and washed it down with coffee. Next time he left Gold Hill he'd have to remember to bring a trail pack. Cody thought about his dilemma, how to escort Talbott's gold with bandits roaming around. After he finished eating he stopped in the saloons seeking Hank. But Hank wasn't there – likely he was still up at the camp. He stopped last in the Tin Cup, Hank's favorite place, and stood at the bar. The night crowd was beginning to come in, and Cody tried to catch the bartender's eye: 'Howdy, Mack.'

'Howdy Cody, what'll you have?'

'I got a quick question for ya, Mack. How did Sheriff Corrigan handle Talbott's shipments before?'

Mack had a puzzled look on his face, 'Don't rightly know what you're saying there, Cody.'

'His gold, Talbott wants to send a wagonload to Denver instead of keeping it in the local bank. He said he did it before, but with the sheriff's help. So what did Corrigan do?'

Mack scratched his face. 'Oh yeah, the gold wagon, I

remember now. That was six months ago, only time Talbott's done it. Ole Joe he rounded up some men he trusted and asked for a contingent of federal marshals from Denver. He had a few connections back there. Anyway, they pulled it off without a hitch. My guess is that Talbott greased his palm a little. Why do you ask?'

' 'Cause Talbott just asked me to do the same thing. Round up a bunch of men and escort his wagon to Denver. Except I don't know anybody well enough to trust them to do that – well, Hank, but that's it.'

'What about the marshals?'

'Too late to ride there and ask them. Talbott wants to move the gold out tomorrow noon.'

'Oh boy, that is a tough one. What you gonna do?'

Cody shrugged his shoulders, 'I reckon I'll just show up tomorrow noon and escort the gold all by my lonesome, and hope for the best.'

'Well good luck, some of them prospectors might have their gold in that wagon too. I hope you don't lose none, they'll be madder than a stirred-up hornet's nest.'

Cody bid Mack good night and went back to the jailhouse to sleep. His instincts told him to run away, to forget his responsibilities, but he knew that was the cowardly Cody talking. He had to face his fears, he couldn't run forever, he'd run out of places to run before too long. No, tomorrow he would face Talbott and escort that gold wagon to Denver all by himself if need be.

CHAPTER 8

Lionel rode back into Gold Hill nonchalantly. Less than a week ago had passed since he had been driven out of town in shame. Now, he returned like a conqueror. It was mid-morning, and in a few hours Julius and his men would come swarming out of the hills to steal the town's gold. His job was to make sure the deputy, the remaining lawman, didn't interfere. He walked into the same saloon he had been caught cheating at cards and sat in a corner, hidden by smoke and shadows, his hat pulled low over his eyes. The place was empty except for the bartender, who busied himself in the back. The gambler settled in and waited; it wouldn't be long now.

Cody woke up early and prepared himself to face Talbott. He checked his Colt to make sure it was ready. He put a bandolier around his belt. There was a Henry rifle Joe kept hidden in a closet that Cody had found, along with an extra box of ammunition for it. He packed a saddlebag and filled his canteen of water. He was ready, prepared to meet any bandits on the road.

Now, he only needed to convince Talbott that he could do the job by himself. Easy enough, he thought.

Checking himself in the mirror one last time, Cody took a deep breath and stepped out into the street. It was ten minutes to noon. The wagon would be in front of the bank, waiting to take the load of gold to Denver. He walked his gelding over, the Henry over his shoulder. As he approached the bank he noticed a blur of motion to his left, in a saloon's doorway. Cody flinched, then saw a man wearing a black hat stepping forward to grab the gelding's reins. Cody recognized him immediately.

'Lionel? I thought the sheriff ran you out?'

'Well, I'm back, and I'm here to tell you to fan the breeze. What's about to happen, you don't want any part of. Now git.' He tugged on the reins. Cody held on tight. The gambler reached for his Remington. Just then a loud 'He-ya!' filled the air, followed by the rumbling noise of hoofs and wheels. Talbott's wagon had arrived. It pulled up short next to the bank, two hundred feet from where Cody and Lionel stood.

The gambler looked Cody in the eyes and said, 'I warned you, coward.' He let go of the reins, defying Cody to draw, his hand still on his Remington. The deputy didn't take the bait, but instead, ignoring Lionel, headed to the wagon. Talbott was already there, directing the bank manager where to put his sacks of gold.

'About time, deputy, where's your posse?' He said without looking at Cody. The gold baron was overseeing three bank employees, plus the driver, hauling the gold out of the bank. Another man, one of Talbott's employees Cody guessed, stood by the wagon – a converted Conestoga, its cloth covering spotted with grime – holding a shotgun. 'No, stack them longways, I don't want any gold dust spilling out.'

'Mr Talbott, sir, I can assure you that the bank vault is safe,' the bank manager said as he tried to get Talbott's attention.

'I doubt that, but it ain't about just being safe. I gotta get this gold to my buyer. Anyway, just load up my gold. Cody, where's your posse?'

'There ain't no posse, Mr Talbott, it's just me. I'll escort your gold to Denver for you.'

The consortium owner gave him an incredulous look, 'By yourself?'

'Who else can you trust?'

Talbott's mouth worked with no sound coming out, then muttering curse words, beat his leg with his hat, while pacing in a circle. 'Don't that beat all? Do I have a choice?'

'Mr Talbott, I could. . . .' the bank manager butted in.

'Shut up, you. Just finish loading up my wagon. Cody, get ready to ride.'

Cody smiled broadly, and patted his gelding, ready to mount up. Then everything started moving fast. Lionel – Cody had forgotten all about the gambler – crept up behind him and hit him hard over the head. The deputy stumbled and fell. He looked up, dazed, and saw Lionel holding his gun, barrel first.

'You have a hard head, that blow should have knocked you out cold! I told you to fan the breeze!'

Before Cody could respond he heard shouts, war whoops from all around. Then a gunshot, and the thundering of hoofs. 'Hold it, hands up, clear of your guns.' It was Lionel. Cody heard another shot, and tried to stand up. 'Stay down if you know what's good for you.' Cody ignored the warning and raised his head, getting to a crouch before he paused. His head was pounding, but he could see straight and what he saw scared the hell out of him. A group of riders appeared as if from nowhere. Cody counted more than twenty. They scattered the few people who were on the street and surrounded the wagon. Cody could see the man with the shotgun lying dead on the ground, the driver's hands were raised, and the bank employees were cowering near the door.

'Thank you kindly for loading our wagon. Make sure the bank is clear, we don't want to leave any gold behind.' The speaker rode a giant black stallion. He had a trim beard, and wielded a sword instead of a revolver, looking more like a cavalry officer than a bank robber.

'A few more sacks to load up, Julius,' said one of his men.

'Get to it,' he roared. 'Time's a-wastin.'

Cody struggled to rise. He was spotted by the cavalry officer. 'Hewitt, shoot that deputy.'

'All the gold is loaded Julius.'

'Let's go, let's go!' The men rode off without hesitation. Two jumped on to the wagon, one grabbing the reins of the team of six horses, while the other covered him with a Henry. Cody could see Talbott standing off to the side, fuming in anger. Less than a minute after they had arrived, the riders were gone, barreling out of town.

'Deputy, my gold. My gold is getting away, stop them!' Cody got up and surveyed the scene. The riders, Lionel among them, were at the edge of town now. The bank manager and his employees were huddled next to the door, while the driver stood next to Talbott who was gesturing at Cody, his face a mask of fury.

'You imbecile, why didn't you stop them?'

'No, I didn't, there were too many, I. . . .' Cody tried to explain, but Talbott wasn't having it.

'Get my gold back now, or there'll be hell to pay.'

More people were coming on to the street. Word would get out to the prospectors in the camp. Some of what was taken was their gold, too. Cody clasped his hands together, realizing then that he was shaking. It seemed just like the war. Running away would be easy, but no, he was done with that, or so he wanted to believe. Talbott was still ranting, drawing more onlookers, while the bank manager tried to calm him. These people depended on him to keep the peace. Cody steeled his resolve.

'I'll get the gold back,' he said in a smaller voice than he meant. He was ignored by everyone. 'I'll get your gold, Mr Talbott. I'll head out right now, while the tracks are still fresh.'

Talbott looked at him, his expression hard. 'You better!' With all eyes on him, Cody mounted his gelding, his head still pounding, and unsteadily trotted after the robbers. There were over twenty of them, too

many for one man to handle alone, but he had to try
something. Cody needed to redeem himself, even if it
meant his own death.

CHAPTER 9

Lionel watched the men transfer the gold from the mule train and the Cripple Creek and Clear Creek robberies to the wagon. There was a military precision to their work. He wasn't told what they did or where they came from, but he always half-suspected they were from the Confederate Army. Julius always struck him as a cavalry officer, more so today with his performance in Gold Hill. Jeffrey, Julius's second-in-command, approached Lionel.

He watched the men in silence for a while then said, 'Quite a load, eh. Julius estimates that between all the banks and mule trains and what not, we've got a ton and a half of pure gold on our hands. Could be less, could be more, but close to a ton and a half, that's 1.2 million dollars. Enough money to buy fifty thousand French troops to help the Confederacy. Well, at least rent them for a while.'

'Fifty thousand troops?'

'Yup, Maximillian's got forty thoussand French, and another ten thousand are scattered around the West

Indies. This is just a down payment, but it's enough to bring them into the war. We gotta haul this all the way to Veracruz though. You coming?'

'Will I get paid?'

'In Veracruz you will.'

'I guess I'm going to Veracruz then.'

Jeffrey smiled and walked away, leaving Lionel alone with his thoughts. Over a million dollars sitting there, enough for him to live comfortably for the rest of his days. Against a less formidable foe Lionel would have chanced stealing at least some of this money, but not against Julius Tucker and his men. They were uncompromising in their steadfast loyalty to the Confederate cause. He could see it in their eyes and their movements; hard men. Not a one would be tempted to help him.

No, better to ride this out and hope they didn't betray him in the end. Lionel turned to leave but his movement caught Julius's attention. The Confederate leader came over to stand next to Lionel, blocking his path. His movements were fluid for such a big man, one moment he was twenty paces away and the next he had covered the distance. Lionel had to look up, the man was a full head taller than him.

'Why didn't you kill that deputy when I asked you to?'

For a moment Lionel was silent – nothing, it seems, escaped Julius's attention. 'You don't need to worry about him,' said Lionel, recovering. 'He's just a coward. He won't trouble us none.'

Julius leaned over and said in a low voice, almost a

whisper, 'You better be right, gambler. We can't afford to have anyone on our back trail. If he finds us, I'll kill him and you.'

Lionel said nothing, only nodding as Julius released his gaze and walked on to another section of the camp. The gambler didn't know why he had let the deputy live, perhaps he had a soft spot for pathetic creatures. Lionel was certain about Cody's cowardice. The deputy wouldn't follow them, rather he would leave town and hide out in the mountains or find another town to hide out in.

Lionel nodded to himself, hoping he was right, but there was a small nagging doubt that he was wrong, and that Cody Black, deputy sheriff, would show up trying to return the gold. He hoped that nagging doubt was just his imagination. He had little doubt that Julius Tucker would carry out his threat to kill him if he ever saw the deputy again.

Cody had little trouble following the trail this time. The wagon was heavy and left deep ruts on the road. He wondered how the robbers would get it into the mountains, to their hideout, without difficulty. Also of concern was what he would do if he got lost again. The wagon tracks were easy now, but if it rained those ruts would be washed out. He paused to take a drink from his canteen. He sat ahorse, only a few miles outside Gold Hill, when he heard a rider coming from behind. Cody pulled the Henry out of its scabbard and aimed it. The rider came from the direction of Gold Hill, so he waited a breath before pulling the trigger. The rider hailed him, and he recognized the voice – Hank. He took the rifle off his shoulder and waited.

Hank rode up to him panting. 'Howdy, Cody. I heard about the gold shipment being stolen. Mind if I ride with you?'

'What fer?' Cody said, his eyes narrowing.

'To be honest, I was sent by Mr Talbott. He said I was to keep an eye on you. I don't think he trusts you none.'

'Is he coming too?'

Hank nodded, 'He's getting together a posse, wants his gold real bad. Said I should go first since you and I are friends and all.'

'Damn, he's gonna make my job harder.'

'What's your play?'

'I'm going on. You wanna come, come, but follow my lead. I'm in charge.'

'You wanna deputize me?'

'I don't have a badge, but I can give you the authority, I guess. Seeing as how I'm acting sheriff until we find out for sure what happened to Sheriff Corrigan.'

'Sounds good, Sheriff,' Hank grinned broadly. Cody just shrugged his shoulders and sighed. 'We got to get to the gold before Talbott does. I don't want a big shoot-out like they had in Clear Creek.'

They moved on in tandem. Hank, a better tracker than Cody, would take point, following the wagon tracks carefully.

'It looks like they're headed to one of the box canyons in the mountains.'

'Where are they?'

'They're all over the place, well hidden little valleys,

and good places to put the wagon.'

Cody thought about that wagon, there was too much gold to haul on horse, and the wagon would slow them down. He wasn't quite sure what he would do once he caught up to them. The posse was on his heels and the matter may soon be taken from him. Still, he couldn't allow a shoot-out. He'd have to play it as it came. Hank was unusually quiet during their journey. He had taken point, for which Cody was grateful. The wagon ruts that were so easy to follow right out of town began disappearing as they headed further into the mountains, and soon they disappeared altogether.

It was almost dark when they came to a wide road. Hank stopped his roan and waited for Cody to catch up. 'This here's the stage road between Denver and the gold towns to the south, Clear Creek and Cripple Creek. It doesn't reach Gold Hill, there's another road that does that, headed north and then east. I reckon we're about twenty miles south of town.'

'So where'd they go?'

Hank shrugged. 'Beats me. I lost the wagon tracks a while ago, but I knew the road was here. I figured we'd come here and pick up the tracks again.'

'It's getting late. We should double back, see if we missed them.'

Hank sighed, 'I'd just as soon as make camp. Can't see nothing in the dark. They can't go too far up here.'

'What about the posse?' Cody asked.

'Who knows? Maybe they'll catch up, or perhaps they caught up to the villains already. Either way let's camp here.'

Cody didn't like that idea, but he kept his mouth shut. There was no point in continuing on at night, if Hank was adamant about stopping. The Texan unsaddled and hobbled his horse, allowing him to graze. Aways from the road there was a little pond that Hank found, so Cody led his gelding there. They ate dried beef without lighting a fire. He and Hank laid out their bedding nearby and Hank soon drifted off to sleep. Cody lay awake looking at the stars, trying to keep his mind a blank, listening to Hank's snores. He was about to drift off when he heard something rustling. His horse whickered, and then more movement.

Not daring to breath, Cody reached for his Colt. He sat up, bringing the Colt up level, to see a cougar staring at him from the edge of the camp. The sleek cat was crouched low, ready to pounce. He aimed his gun and prepared to shoot. In the dim light he'd be lucky to hit it. For a brief moment time seemed to stand still. Cody held his breath, the mountain lion raised its head, sniffing the wind. Then he stood up and ambled away, unhurried. Cody didn't realize his hands were sweaty. The animals were scarier than the men in this wild country, so far anyway, and the woods were full of them. He'd be glad when the dawn came. Cody slept fitfully that night, keeping one hand on his Dragoon.

CHAPTER 10

The men had worked through the afternoon loading and securing all the gold. They broke camp just as the sun set. Julius had thought traveling at night would be better, to put some distance between them and Gold Hill before the law got organized. 'I suspect they'll send a posse after us.' Julius had said. 'That Yankee dandy didn't look too happy we absconded with his gold. Watch our back trail Hewitt, that's your job.' Lionel resigned himself to his duty when the Confederates rolled out at dusk. In hiding the wagon from the inevitable pursuit Julius had several of his men tie tree branches behind their horses. When the wagon veered off the path, to their hidden encampment, they swept in from behind and obliterated the wagon tracks. Once the wagon was hidden, they cut away the branches and kept riding on to lead the pursuit away. The men, ten of them, would meet up with the rest somewhere down south. It was a brilliant plan, Lionel thought, and more evidence that Julius was a cavalry officer.

Lionel was sympathetic to the Confederate cause, he was a Missourian, a border state, which lent him some credibility in these men's eyes. But ultimately he was a pragmatist, who cared only for himself. He saw the Confederates losing, and that instilled a wild desperation in these men. He didn't think their plan would work, but knew he couldn't convince them otherwise. Instead he would go along, and if the law or the Union Army caught up with them he would hightail it. Make for California, or even Canada if need be. He had his skill with the gun and the luck of the cards. It was dark now and he couldn't see, and had to trust his horse not to lose his footing. He could hear the wagon creak as it lumbered on. The noise was lulling him to sleep, but he started when a voice whispered in his ear.

'Nice way to watch our back trail,' said Jeffrey. 'We're almost to the south road, then we'll be able to cover more ground. We'll meet up with Beau's group in the foothills there. Don't fall asleep or I'll tan your hide.' Jeffrey gave Lionel a meaningful look and the gambler only nodded. Lionel was half tempted to leave these men to their fate if he continued to receive tongue lashings from Jeffrey, or his boss Julius. The gambler took a deep breath once Jeffrey moved ahead to the front of the column. His pride was one thing, the gold he was promised at the end was another. Better to stick it out, he told himself, then I can put a bullet in one of these Confederate officers if he irks me again. He smiled at the thought. It comforted him, and kept him awake through the night.

*

Cody was up early and saw that Hank had already made breakfast. If jerky and hard biscuits could be called breakfast. They saddled up and rode out. Hank, riding next to Cody, leaned over and said, 'We'll follow the road a bit, see if the wagon made it here. If not we can double back. Did you hear anything during the night?'

'Only a mountain lion who wanted to eat me for his dinner.'

'Heh, you gotta be careful out here. This ain't Ohio.'

No, it isn't that, Cody thought, but left the words unsaid. Instead, he wondered where the outlaws had gone – or, for that matter, the posse.

'There were tracks that led down to the south,' Hank said when asked by Cody. 'Maybe they went that way. Must have passed us, or they're still further back – takes a while to get a posse together.'

Cody only nodded. After a few hours he could see a thin line of smoke filling the air. 'Something up ahead,' said Hank, and he kicked at his roan, urging it on faster. Cody withdrew his Henry and held it on his lap as he matched Hank's speed. Before long they saw the cause of the smoke: a burned-out stage lying on its side right off the road.

Cody and Hank approached cautiously. There were two bodies lying next to the stage, shot up. The team was cut away and was grazing nearby, unconcerned. Then Cody heard the click of a hammer being drawn back, and froze. 'Don't, don't move, I've got you covered.' It was a high-pitched, feminine voice. Hank and Cody both raised their hands. A woman, her blonde hair waving in the wind, her face dirty, came out

66

from behind a thicket of trees, a rifle pointed right at them. 'Who are you?' she asked, trying to keep the terror from her voice.

'We're just passing through, ma'am, we saw the smoke and thought you might need help. What happened?' Hank said.

The woman seemed hesitant, and then Cody said 'I'm a sheriff's deputy, ma'am, from Gold Hill, we aren't bandits. My name's Cody, and this here is Hank. We're here to help.' He pointed to his star. Her face flooded with relief.

'Oh, thank goodness, I was sure you were coming back to rob me. A group of men, they came on us early this morning. At least ten, or fifteen even. They were traveling with a wagon.'

'A wagon, you say?' Cody leaned in, his interest keen.

'Yes, a wagon. I was headed to Clear Creek for, for work in the saloon, and these men, some of them came up and started shooting, they killed the driver and another passenger. They would have hurt me or worse, but then one man on a huge black horse stopped them. He seemed to be their leader. They listened to him well enough. They were well disciplined, almost like soldiers. Anyway, they looted the stage and set it on fire. They let me go with a warning, not to tell anyone about them. Then they left. I took the driver's rifle and hid in the woods in case they came back.'

'Which way did they go?'

'South, toward Clear Creek I reckon.'

'That's our quarry Cody, let's get them.'

'What about this lady? What's your name, ma'am?'

'Susan, but you can call me Sue.'

'We have to go, Cody.'

'I'm not leaving her behind. It's my duty as a lawman. Sue, ma'am, why don't you come with us? We'll catch up one of those horses for you to ride.'

'Thank you, Cody, but there's no saddle and I'm not a very good rider.'

Cody scratched his head. 'All right, you'll ride double with me. It'll slow us down, sure. . .' Cody gave Hank a look, daring him to speak out, '. . .but that's fine. We'll get you to Clear Creek or somewhere safe.'

Sue smiled. Her blue eyes were bright, her smile warm, inviting. 'Thank you Deputy Cody, that is most thoughtful of you.' Hank gave him a sour look but said nothing as he helped Sue on to the back of the gelding.

'I can come back for my things. I want to be out of these dreadful woods.'

Cody clucked, and the gelding moved on. Hank, somber, followed, his own horse moving slowly. There was still no sign of the outlaws, and Cody tried to mask his uneasiness as Sue put her hands around his waist.

Clear Creek was a town in chaos. When the trio arrived they saw people running to and fro carrying sacks, two brawls in the street, and gunshots coming from the saloon.

'What in tarnation's happening here?' asked Hank.

'The town lost its sheriff a while back, killed by the same gang we're tracking, I suspect.'

'Cody's right, Hank – the other passenger who was traveling with me was supposed to be Clear Creek's new sheriff. He's dead now,' Sue added quietly.

'You can't stay here Sue, these men will only have their way with you with no law in town. You're safer with us.'

'Cody, where we're going is too dangerous to bring a woman.'

'Hank, we've got to bring her. She's under my protection now. We'll take her . . . we'll take her to Cripple Creek. How about that?'

Hank gave a snort, but said nothing. But Cody meant what he said: he wanted to keep Sue protected – besides, he liked having her around, though he would never admit it.

'Thank you, Deputy Cody, but I can take care of myself. I have a contract with the saloon owner, a Mr Harvey Davis. I'm sure he will keep me under his protection.'

Cody gave a slow nod. 'If'n you say so Miss Sue. But if this Harvey Davis turns out to be a lowdown snake I feel it is my duty to escort you to Cripple Creek, Ma'am.'

Sue smiled, and the three of them rode to the saloon, where they had heard gunshots. Inside, the aftermath of a fight was being mopped up. A heavyset man wearing an apron was sweeping the floor. His hair was long and unkempt, like his beard. He looked up and eyed the newcomers, his gaze lingering on Sue.

Cody cleared his throat. 'We're looking for Harvey Davis. You him?'

'Who wants to know?'

'I'm Deputy Cody Black from Gold Hill, my friend

Hank, and this is Miss Susan. . . .'

'Egbert, Susan Egbert. I am under contract to Mr Harvey Davis, here.' She offered the man a folded piece of paper.

The man looked at it, his eyes dull. He jerked his head. 'Harvey's in the back. Come with me.' The trio followed to a back door; the barkeep banged on the door once, and then poked his head in. 'Boss, someone here to see you.' He pushed the door open, allowing Cody, Sue and Hank to enter. They saw a thin man, clean shaven, dressed in black, sitting at a table covered with ledgers. He looked up but didn't say anything.

'Mr Davis, I'm Susan Egbert, you bought my contract to work in your saloon.'

Harvey Davis gave a small smile. 'Ah, Miss Egbert, I was wondering when you would arrive. Who are these gentlemen?'

'These men found me on the road after our stage was ambushed. They rescued me. Er, this is Deputy Cody Black, and Hank. . . .'

'Grimes,' said Hank.

'Howdy, thank you for delivering me my property. Now Sue, why don't you go upstairs and see Selena. She'll get you fixed up right and proper. Gentlemen.' Harvey gave a malicious smile and turned back to his ledgers.

Cody's stomach churned. He hadn't realized until now what type of work Sue was contracted for. Now, the realization was burning him up inside. He longed to throttle Harvey, but Hank was tugging on his arm. 'Time to go. We don't want trouble here. Let's go before the gold gets away. She'll be fine.'

But Cody couldn't let it go. He didn't want Sue, a woman he found himself attracted to, working for a man like Harvey Davis. 'Miss Egbert is coming with us, you villainous scoundrel. She isn't going to work for you at all.' Cody lunged forward, and Harvey sat up, taken aback by Cody's tone and aggressive manner. The deputy was about to reach for the saloon owner when he felt a heavy blow on the back of his head. He fell to the floor and knew nothing more.

CHAPTER 11

Lionel tried to sleep, but it was hard to do in the daytime. Julius had his men sleep in shifts, some would watch the road for pursuit, while the rest slept. They had camped not far from the road, hidden by brush, due to concerns that the wagon's axles might break. It had been slow going during the night, so much so that Julius had ordered only one more night of travel. For that Lionel was grateful – he didn't want to sleep during the day. So far there had been no sign of pursuit.

'It looks like Beau did his job and led those buffoons away from us. One last night of riding and then we'll be clear of them,' Julius had said. Lionel didn't know how much of that he believed, but he knew better than to argue. Once they met up with Beau and his ten men the plan was to ride south through New Mexico Territory to Fort Bliss. From there they'd cross over to Mexico, and deliver the gold. It was five hundred miles, at least a week with a wagon, two if they were cautious. A lot could still go wrong. There were Union soldiers, roving bands of Comanche, Cheyenne and

72

Kiowa, other *banditos*, not to mention the pursuit behind them. The gambler hoped they would get there soon.

The day was long, and Lionel eventually did find some sleep. That night the group rode out again, Lionel keeping to his usual place in the rear. He could feel them lose height as they rode: soon they would be out of these mountains. It was almost dawn when the call came from ahead, that riders were approaching. Lionel tensed, fingering his Remington. 'It's Beau, they made it back,' Jeffery shouted back. Good, he thought, now we can get some distance between us and these mining towns. The gambler urged his mount forward to see what news Beau had.

'There were a bunch of them, twenty or more. I lost five men, but we rained a hail of fire on them. Ambushed them in a canyon. They couldn't withstand our Southern fury. Nothing but miners and drifters, they scattered into the mountains. Then we came to find you.' Beau said between gulps of air.

'You weren't followed?'

'No, Col . . . Julius. I'm sure of it.'

Julius nodded, 'Those men will be remembered for their sacrifice. Come on, let's go, by the end of the day we should be on the plains, we can run the wagon there.'

Lionel wondered at the accuracy of Beau's statement. Oh, he was sure there was a firefight, but Beau's group was outnumbered by at least two to one. He wasn't convinced that the posse had run for the hills. It was time he told Julius his misgivings, since his own life was on the line. 'Julius, a word if I may.'

Julius scowled at Lionel's audacity. Jeffrey put a hand on his shoulder, and said 'What is it, gambler? Be quick.'

Lionel plowed ahead. 'Are we so certain that the posse has been so dispersed? How do we know they won't regroup if what Beau said actually happened?'

Julius's eyes bulged, and his face turned red. It was all Jeffrey could do to keep the Confederate cavalry commander from drawing his sidearm. 'I don't doubt my man's assessment of the battle. The posse is disbursed, the rabble could not withstand against Confederate mettle. They won't venture after us again. You, on the other hand, dare doubt the word of a Southern gentleman? You lowdown snake, I have a good mind to thrash you right now.

Lionel held up his hands, 'I'm only saying that as a precaution we should be wary, keep a rearguard still.'

'Fine, you do it then, if you are so concerned. Jeffrey says you are still useful, and we owe you for your assistance so far. But mark me, Missourian, my patience wears thin with you. One more misstep, one more slander, or one more sideways look, and I won't hesitate to put a bullet in your head. Speak naught to me again unless you have something worthwhile to say.' The big Confederate wheeled his horse and yelled for the wagon to get moving. 'We won't rest until tonight.'

Lionel sat, unmoved, while the column moved out. He chewed on his bottom lip, flexing his right hand. Never before had he been spoken to in this manner and allowed the man to live. Now, he was sure of it. He had become weary of the browbeating these Confederate officers were giving him. He would kill Julius once he was paid. If the fool braggart couldn't keep his mouth shut, he might kill him before, even though it would mean his death.

Cody awoke to find himself strapped to his horse's saddle. His head was pounding. The rocking motion of the horse didn't make his headache any easier. He raised his head to see that his gelding was walking along a trail, tied to another horse ridden by Hank. 'What did you do? What happened? Where is Sue?'

Hank turned in his saddle. 'Ah, you're awake, and with so many questions. As to the first and second questions, I hit you over the head with the butt of my revolver. Then, with assistance from our friendly barman I tied you to your saddle where you now find yourself. As to Sue, I imagine she is where we left her.'

Cody struggled to get up, 'Why did you do that? We need to go back and get her.'

Hank's eyes narrowed. 'What for? You have to focus on the task at hand. That floozy has your head a-spinning. If I hadn't intervened you might be dead, and that gold you were entrusted to protect, gone, like the wind.' Hank opened his hand and blew on his palm.

'She's not a floozy,' Cody said, his voice soft, as Hank untied him from the saddle. Once free, and now in a sitting position with Hank an arm's length away, Cody balled his fist and swung hard, hitting Hank square in the face. The Texan reeled backward and fell off his horse.

'That's for calling her a floozy, and for hitting me.'

Hank was on his feet in a flash, crouched in a fighting stance. Then, his anger dissipated, he laughed. Wiping his face clean of blood, he said 'Now that's the spirit I've been looking for, Cody. Like when you pummeled Eaton back at the mining camp. I need your help, Cody. This isn't just for Talbott. That wagon had my gold on it too. My life savings. Prospecting is hard work, and I don't want to start over. I need my gold back, and I can't do it alone. That woman, Sue, I'm sorry I called her a floozy, but she would only distract you. And I can't have you distracted. After this is over you can go back to Clear Creek for all I care, but *after* I have my gold. Agreed?'

Cody stared at the Texan for a long while, then he nodded his head. 'All right Hank, I see what you mean. I guess I got a little carried away by her. You could have just told me, you didn't have to knock me out.'

'It was the only way to get through to you.'

Cody didn't respond, but moved his gelding forward. He was surprised by his own actions in the saloon. Since he deserted he had tried to avoid conflict. His fight with Eaton had been out of self-defence, but this was the first time he had initiated action. That woman, Sue, had done something to him. She was different, someone worth fighting for. Or so he had convinced himself. But Hank was right, he hated to admit it, she would have been a distraction. The wagon and recovery of the stolen gold took precedence. It was the only thing that mattered, not only for Hank, but for himself as well, for redemption. He couldn't allow himself to become distracted again.

Hank took point as they rode. There was no sign of the wagon, but Hank surmised they would be heading south, out of the mountains. Cody didn't disagree. Before long Hank stopped his horse: he was peering down at the ground, looking intently. 'There are many tracks here, no wagon, but a heck of a mess of hoof prints. Let's see where they lead.'

'Sounds good, keep your sidearm ready, just in case.' Cody pulled out the Henry. The tracks, Cody could see them now, led off the road. He wondered if this was the posse or the outlaws. It didn't take long to find out. The tracks led to a small canyon. Dead bodies of men and horses littered the floor. A shoot-out.

'Damnation, I recognize some of these men. This is the posse,' said Hank as he got off his horse for a closer look.

'They must have found the outlaws.'

'That they did, Cody, that they did. Or at least some of them.'

Cody froze as he heard a clicking sound, a rifle being cocked. 'Hands in the air, stay right where you are.' Both Hank and Cody did as the voice commanded. Instantly, riders appeared out of the brush.

'It's all right, it's only Hank. And the deputy.'

Talbott rode up on a big dun. 'Well, bless my soul, it's about time you two showed up here. Taking in the scenery, or were you too afraid to face the gunfire?'

'We were tracking the wagon but we lost it.'

Talbott put up a hand, 'The wagon's not here. We were tricked. Rode right into an ambush. They used boulders and cut down trees and laid down one round of fire, then they hightailed it.'

'Which way?'

Talbott gave Cody a look, with a raised eyebrow. 'If I knew that, deputy, we'd be in pursuit. As it stands we had to tend our wounded and regroup. Then we lost the trail. One of our scouts spotted riders coming, so we hid, figuring they were coming back. Didn't expect to see you. I thought you had fanned the breeze already.'

'Talbott, I'm the law in Gold Hill. At least until a new sheriff is appointed, or Sheriff Corrigan returns.'

'We found Corrigan's body, strung up in a small gulch near Gold Hill.'

'Well, that just confirms it then, I am the law,' Cody said with a shaky voice.

'Then act like it and find my wagon.'

'I'll find the gold. Just stay out of my way.' Cody spurred his horse on, trying to get away from the stares of Talbott and his posse. 'I hope that lights a fire under him,' he heard Talbott say. 'We can't rely on him, though. Come on boys, let's find my wagon, and get our gold back.' Cody kept riding on until he was out of earshot. He didn't even know if Hank was following him. He didn't care. They were all against him, but he would find that wagon and rescue the gold if it was the last thing he ever did.

CHAPTER 12

Cody hadn't gone far when he heard a horse whinny behind him. He saw it was Hank, and greeted him with 'I was wondering when you'd show up.'

'Can't let you have all the fun. Besides, what would you do without me?'

Cody halted his horse until Hank was alongside him.

'I'm sorry Hank, I needed to get away from Talbott. Some of the things he said were true – too true, in fact.'

'What do you mean?'

Cody looked at his friend, perhaps the only friend he had left in the world, and said, 'Hank, I'm a coward. I was with the Army of the Tennessee and there was a battle, and I couldn't take it. My best friend, Tommy Gill, I saw him get shot and skewered by a bayonet. So I turned tail and ran, in the heat of battle. I couldn't fight any more. I ran and didn't stop till I got to Gold Hill. So here I am, not only a deserter, but a coward too. Kind of ironic that I'm a lawman now, huh?'

For a long moment Hank didn't say anything, and

Cody feared that he had angered his friend with his revelation. Then Hank pushed his hat back on his head and said, 'That's quite a tale. I, too, was supposed to fight, for the Confederacy and Texas, but I feel no particular allegiance to either. So I left, before I could be corralled into joining the army. Might not have made my ma and pa too proud, but so be it. I'm making my own fortune in life.'

His parents: Cody had forgotten about his own parents, or at least had tried to. Simple farm folk, whose oldest son was off to war. He wondered if he would ever be able to face them again. A thought for another day, perhaps. He pushed his family from his mind, focusing on the present. He bent over the gelding's neck, but could see no tracks.

'According to Talbott, these bandits that surprised him didn't leave any noticeable tracks. They are real good, whoever they are,' said Hank.

'Skilled at arms and laying ambushes, disciplined, almost like an army. Now they're carrying a heap of gold, with robberies in multiple towns, if these are the same crooks who hit Clear Creek. And headed south.' South, there was nothing. They were past Pike's Peak. Everything beyond this was just grasslands, a few ranches and cow towns, and New Mexico Territory. New Mexico Territory, where the Apache were, Texas, where the Confederates were, and Mexico, where French and Mexican troops were. Cody, his eyes wide, had a sudden revelation, and told Hank his theory:

'Hold your horses, Hank, I think I know where they're going. These aren't any run-of-the-mill outlaws, they're Confederates, and they want the gold to help the war cause.'

'Now ain't that something! Maybe that's true, but what do you reckon to do about it?'

'Head them off. While Talbott and his men muck around here, we'll head for New Mexico Territory. The Union Army has a presence there now. We could enlist their help.'

'With you, a deserter?'

'Yeah, that's where you come in Hank,' said Cody, his voice small.

Hank scratched his chin, then nodded, 'Let's do it Cody, let's get that gold back.'

For the first time in what seemed like ages Cody smiled, and it was a smile filled with hope and relief. Perhaps he could do it, find the gold, stop a mad Confederate plot to turn the war, and redeem himself. It was still a long shot, and first they had to get ahead of the gang. Abruptly he changed direction, heading east away from the setting sun. 'Let's make up as much ground as we can before it gets dark.' Enough ground to leave Talbott in the dust and make ground on the Confederates.

Early the next day the duo left the mountainous terrain behind, and as they rode out of the foothills a vast plain opened up before them. 'We should make better time now,' said Hank. Since they had left Gold Hill they had seen no sign of the wagon. They had either come out ahead of it or they still needed to catch up. Speed was of the essence, as the Union Army had to be involved if these bandits were Confederates.

Cody didn't want to overwork his horse, but wanted him to run a little, so he clicked him from a trot to a canter. Hank kept pace. Switching back to a trot, then again to canter, the pair made up the ground between them and their quarry.

After noon, Cody spied a cloud of dust in the distance. Riders. He wondered if this was their mark. He signaled Hank to slow down, and pulled his own horse into a trot. 'Let's not get too close, until we know if they're friendly or not.'

Cody wanted to wait until nightfall before he got close to the group ahead of them. He knew that they were far enough away not to have noticed the two riders behind them. 'What do you want to do, Cody?' Hank asked, as Cody had stopped his horse completely.

'Let's wait until they make camp. Then we'll see if these are our bandits.' Cody gigged his mount into a trot again as the cloud of dust faded. The group, whoever they were, was moving fast. For several hours Cody and Hank shadowed them, just keeping the cloud of trail dust in view. Cody guessed he and Hank were a couple of miles behind the group of riders, too far for them to be seen. As dusk began to settle Cody urged his gelding forward at a faster pace, thinking that the party ahead would begin to make camp. But they didn't. Hank was getting too close, and Cody had to whistle to him to fall back. The pair rode off the trail into some brush to let the other group get ahead. Cody could make out the outline of a wagon in the fading sunlight surrounded by riders. Yes, he thought, this was them. But they weren't stopping, which caused him some concern.

'Cody. . . .' the unspoken question hung in the air between them.

'I know Hank, but they'll stop soon. They have to. They've got to rest their horses. Just be patient and keep following them. We can get a little bit closer now that the sun is almost down.' The two edged forward out of the grass and back on the trail, the wagon and its riders now ahead in the distance. Cody heard fading hoofbeats as they rode, then they were gone. The sun had now completely set and the birds had gone quiet.

There was no sound on the prairie save for the occasional yip of a coyote. Cody reasoned the group had at last stopped for the night – but where? He and Hank kept riding, but he didn't know if the group was still ahead of them, or if they had passed them in the dark. Cody stopped and dismounted. 'Been a long day, might want to give the horses a rest.' Hank nodded and dismounted as well.

'Where are they?'

'Don't know, they're slippery though. Let's keep looking, then we'll make camp.'

But as Cody started to move a gunshot sliced through the air. Instinctively Cody hit the dirt, letting go of the gelding's reins. The horse jumped and ran off into the night. Cody cursed – his Henry was still on his saddle. All he had left was the Dragoon. He unholstered his gun and looked around for Hank. He saw his friend lying face down in the dirt, his horse also missing. A moment of panic gripped the deputy and he rolled the Texan over. 'You OK?'

'I'm all right, but I think the bullet nicked my leg.'

Another shot hit the dirt near them, and Cody braced his friend. 'We've got to go. Can you move?'

'I'll try.' Hank began to crawl, his left leg immobile behind him. The two of them crawled into deep grass. Two more shots flew above them. Cody froze, knowing they couldn't outpace the shooter. He waved Hank to stop moving. If they played dead the gunman would get up close and Cody could take him, or so the deputy hoped. They were deep enough in the thick grass to hide in the twilight. Cody held his breath, Hank was still behind him. The deputy hoped his friend hadn't passed out. Soon he heard footsteps, someone approaching. Cody readied his Dragoon, keeping his breathing as light as possible. He heard the hammer being pulled back on a gun, and heavy breathing.

'Deputy, is that you?' A boot came hard into Cody's ribs, forcing him to grunt and roll over. 'Why, yes it is. I thought you were the one following us.' Cody recognized the voice as belonging to Lionel Hewitt, the gambler. Cody lifted his Dragoon, but Lionel was quicker, his Navy already leveled at Cody. 'None of that now, deputy. I let you live once, much to the chagrin of my employer. If he finds out I let you live a second time I might find myself dead. He is a harsh, unforgiving man, more dedicated to his cause than anything.'

'The Confederacy?'

Hewitt clapped one hand lightly against his thigh, the gun still aimed at Cody. 'Yes, you've figured it out. Now as I was saying, drop your gun, and maybe I'll let your friend live.' Cody tossed his gun at the gambler. As

Hewitt smiled, Hank, silently crawling through the grass, made his move, grabbing Lionel by the ankles, tripping him. His arms akimbo, the Navy Remington went wide. Cody wasted no time, scooping up a handful of dirt and tossing it into Lionel's eyes. He grabbed his Dragoon and kicked Lionel for good measure. 'Come on Hank, grab my arm. We've got to get out of here, in case there are more.' Cody picked up his friend and dragged him away from the still thrashing gambler.

Lionel wiped the dirt from his eyes then groped around for his gun. He was surprised to still be alive. Perhaps the deputy wanted to return the favor Lionel had granted him back in Gold Hill. More likely, though, he was worried about Lionel's confederates in the area. He smiled at his pun. This deputy sheriff was becoming a nuisance. He should have killed him when he had the chance instead of being so overconfident. Next time he'll just kill them both. He hoped the camp hadn't heard the gunshots. It was far enough away that he didn't think so, but even so, he would still tell Julius and Jeffrey he was scaring away a coyote.

Now Lionel needed to track down the deputy. His friend was wounded, he knew that for certain, so they could not go far. Not for the first time he wished he had a rifle. But his Navy Remington had been with him through more than one scrape, and he trusted it to do the job. He just needed to sneak up on them and get real close.

Stealthily, he moved through the tall grass. He didn't hear the rustling that he expected from his escaping quarry. Instead, it was eerily quiet. Lionel crouched down in the grass wondering if Hank was going to try and trip him again. He wouldn't fall for that trick again. Then he heard the grass rustling: his mark was moving. Lionel stood up as the noise became louder, coming closer. Too late he turned around to see the butt end of a Henry smack him in the face. Lionel ducked, softening the blow, but it wasn't enough for him to keep his balance. Down he went, and a hail of punches followed – it was all he could do to cover his head, until one haymaker knocked him out cold.

CHAPTER 13

When he came to, Lionel found himself trussed up like a hog waiting for slaughter. His hands were behind his back and his feet were bound, but he wasn't gagged or blindfolded. It was also morning. Dang, he thought, that deputy got the drop on me. He tried to stand up but his legs were too hobbled and he only succeeded in falling over. He rolled over on his back, breathing heavily. He thought about revenge against the deputy and his friend. Twice he had let him live when he should have killed him. There wouldn't be a third time. The gambler spent most of the morning trying to get free of his bonds. He writhed on the ground looking for any sharp stone or stick or hard surface that could be used. It took several hours and many attempts to cut away the tied rope. His hands bled from the effort, and ached as he untied his legs.

His would-be captors had not made the knots extremely tight, just enough to keep him waylaid for a while. His Remington was gone, though, which didn't surprise him. His hands still ached from being tied and his legs were numb. Lionel walked in a circle, getting the blood flowing back into his extremities. He wondered if the deputy had found his horse, hidden in a nearby meadow.

Lionel was lucky – the claybank was grazing contentedly when he found him. He searched his saddle-bag and brought out his canteen; he took a big swig of water from it, and then brought out his spare Remington. It was a twin to the one he always carried, but one he kept hidden just in case. Now ready, he jumped on to his still saddled horse. But before he could return to the Confederates he needed to kill the deputy, and get his gun back.

Cody watched his friend sway in his saddle. It was no good, he couldn't let Hank continue riding with him. 'Hank, old buddy, you don't look so good. Is that bullet still in your leg?' Cody had done his best to staunch the blood flow and clean the wound, but Hank still looked pale.

'I think the bullet just grazed me, I'll be fine.'

Cody looked skeptical. 'You gotta get some help. Maybe there's a homestead around here where we can stop and you can rest for a while.'

'No way Cody, I'm with you all the way.'

Cody paused, contemplating what to do. They had found the camp of riders, but had kept their distance, circling around. Cody wanted to make sure that Lionel didn't raise an alarm if he made it back to the camp. He should have killed the bastard gambler when he'd had the chance, but hadn't wanted to risk a gunshot in case they were close to the Confederates. Beating the man to death seemed senseless, so Cody had done the next best thing, which was to tie him up and take his gun.

The camp had broken early, with military precision. Cody and Hank had found a low rise fairly close, but still far enough away that they wouldn't be seen – or so he hoped, at least. Now that the camp was discovered, Cody was unsure of what to do. There were too many men for him and Hank to take them. He counted at least twenty horses, plus the wagon. And there was the fact that Hank was weakened from his wound, in no shape to fight, despite his bluster. The group was moving out, and Cody's only hope was to shadow them and wait to see if an opportunity came up. But he was worried about Hank, something had to be done. His mind made up, he whistled for the gelding to trot. 'We'll head north for now, Hank. We know where they're going, so they won't get far. There's nowhere they can hide out here, so we can go a roundabout way.'

'To cut them off?'

'Yeah. But for now we'll try to find a homestead or somewhere for you to lay up for a spell.'

'I told ya, Cody, I'm fine.'

'Plus, we need more men if we're gonna take down that gang.'

'Nah, the two of us will be enough. Just let me at 'em for stealing my gold!'

Cody smiled at his friend's bravado. No, he had already watched one friend die in senseless violence. There was no need to risk Hank's life. Going north, northeast, would buy them some time. If they came across a homestead or a small settlement, even better. In addition to Hank's wound being tended they would need supplies, and any men who would volunteer to help them. Now he wondered what had happened to Talbott's posse, if they were still in the mountains or if they had headed south, as the deputy had.

At first Cody had wanted nothing to do with Talbott and the posse. He told himself it was because he was wary of any men getting hurt, but if he was being honest he didn't want Talbott to take over. Cody felt humiliated by what had transpired when he was deputy in Gold Hill: seeing Lionel run out of town after he had let the gambler stay, his failure to stop a street duel, and then seeing all the bank's gold stolen right out from under his nose. He craved redemption, so he needed to do this by himself, without Talbott's interference or abuse. Now, however, Cody regretted not having those men at his disposal.

Too late, he would have to make do with what he had. And what he had was a wounded Hank. He gigged his gelding into a canter and kept going. The riders and wagon were almost out of sight, and Cody wanted to be able to find them again when they headed back south. He knew the army had a presence in the area, but for now Cody wanted to avoid them, at least until Hank was ready. So northeast it was.

Cody let Hank take point, watching him closely. Despite his friend's protestations Cody knew Hank needed to rest. The bullet, or at least a shard, was still in his leg. The bleeding had stopped, but it was becoming discolored, and Cody worried about gangrene. He had seen it enough in the war, and he didn't want his only friend to lose his leg. Still, the Texan was game, and didn't complain.

The plains of Colorado were dotted with small homesteads, folks trying to earn a meager living farming what crops they could. On his way west he had avoided these small farms, fearing retribution for his cowardice. Cody realized now that it was guilt that made him shun any human contact. The wounds from the war were too raw then. Now, though, he had a chance for redemption. A purpose, a mission, he could point the homesteaders to show he backed a cause worth fighting for.

Then late in the afternoon the pair saw signs of civilized life: a thin pillar of smoke rising in the distance. Cody hoped it was from a chimney. As they got closer he could see that it did indeed come from a chimney of a large ranch house. Smiling, he gigged his horse up past Hank. 'Come on Hank, let's see if they're friendly. I wonder if we'll get to eat biscuits.' Hank gave a wan smile, but said nothing.

Cody reached the house and gave a shout: 'Hello there, anybody home?'

A man came out with a shotgun held to his shoulder. 'What do you want?' His voice was gruff, his facial expression hard.

'My friend needs help. Caught a bullet in the leg.'

'Comanche, Cheyenne, or Kiowa?'

'Confederates.'

'Ain't no Confederates around here.'

'Bandits then, maybe they're ex-Confederates. Please, he needs help, can you oblige?'

'Who's asking?'

'Deputy Sheriff Cody Black. I'm from Gold Hill.'

The man scratched his beard. 'Long way away.'

'We're chasing the bandits that shot at him.'

The man stood in the doorway for a while. Cody could almost see him thinking.

Reaching a decision, he nodded. 'All right, you can come. Let me see your badge, though.'

Cody tossed him his star.

'OK, come on in. The missus will see to your friend's wound. Coffee?'

It had been days since Cody had drunk a cup of coffee. He sat down near the kitchen while the man poured himself and Cody a cup, and a middle-aged blonde woman ushered Hank to a bed. When the homesteader said nothing, just sitting and staring at Cody, the deputy swallowed hard and said. 'So what's your name?'

'My name's my business, not yours.'

'I told you mine.'

'That's your problem.' The homesteader said with a snort. The man grew silent, and Cody didn't push the matter. Instead they sat in silence for what seemed like an eternity. After Cody's second cup was drained, the woman came back into the main room. 'Your friend will be fine. There was a piece of metal, a bullet, lodged in his leg. I got it out and cleaned and dressed the wound. He should rest.'

'I'm much obliged ma'am, sir. If Hank can stay here for a few days that would be appreciated. I've got to track. . . .'

'He leaves in the morning, with you.'

'But he can't travel. He needs rest,' Cody began to stammer.

The man's jaw set hard, and through clenched teeth he said, 'I've done my duty to the law. Helping a lawman, if you are who you say you are. Now it's time for you and your friend to leave. He'll live, right, Mama?'

'Yes, Papa, he'll be fine.'

'In the morning you're off my property. You can sleep here in the common room or in the stables with the horses. Your friend can stay in the spare room.' With that, the homesteader walked away, followed by his demure wife. Cody didn't push the issue. He was grateful that Hank would be all right.

As the last rays of the sun glinted over the horizon, Cody saw to the horses, watering them and stabling them, making sure they would be fresh for tomorrow's ride. As he stepped back on to the porch to head back inside he scanned the horizon. He had the vague sense that he was being watched. The deputy wondered if Lionel had broken free and followed them. Cody put the thought from his mind, he was getting too jumpy. The deputy closed the door and slept in the uncomfortable common-room chair so generously offered by the homesteader with no name.

CHAPTER 14

The next day Cody and Hank rode out with the coming dawn. They had been offered a sparse breakfast and some trail vitals by the wife. The husband had gone out early to tend to his chores. The woman smiled pleasantly enough while fixing the food, but she was as communicative as her husband about who they were. Cody could understand, with a war and rebellion, and with hostile Indians roaming around, that a lone homestead was extremely vulnerable. As they rode out Cody spied the farmer, an axe in hand, staring at them as they left. The deputy wanted to tip his hat, but the man's eyes were dark and cold. Involuntarily, a chill went up his spine. Best to be gone from this place, he thought. They rode south now; Cody wanted to make up some time and get closer to the bandits. If Hank was all right, he could ride on to the nearest Union outpost and enlist their aid. But first they had to catch up to the Confederates, and this was no easy task, as the trail had gone cold. But Cody knew they had to keep south to get to Mexico as fast as possible.

The duo made good time. Hank's leg was still weak, but more color had returned to his face and he was more talkative. Cody was hopeful his friend would make a full recovery. He was starting to think things were looking up, when he saw riders coming hard toward them. Cody reined up and signaled to Hank, who nodded.

Neither of them had been paying attention to the road, thinking their quarry was far ahead. Now, Cody saw five riders headed straight toward them. It was too late to run, so the deputy motioned Hank to wait, his hand close to his Colt. The riders bore down hard and then reined up a few feet in front of them. They were a motley lot, wearing mismatched and ragged clothing. Drifters, Cody thought, or perhaps deserters. He swallowed hard at the thought. The lead rider leered at him, his teeth rotten.

'Where are you fer?'

'We're headed south. You?'

The man just stared and spat tobacco juice, and then his eyes narrowed as he focused on Cody's lapel. 'A lawdog!' Cody wore his star openly, but now he cursed – these men were trouble. The rider reached for his belt, but Cody was faster, pointing his Dragoon right at the man's face. 'Don't reach for your iron. I ain't after you. I don't care what you've done, I'm after someone else. You can go, be on your way, and I'll forget I ever saw you.'

Cody hoped he sounded convincing; the last thing

he wanted was a gunfight with these drifters. The rider stared at Cody for a long while, his hand hovering over his sidearm, unmoving. 'Kill 'em Emmet, he's lying,' one of the other men said. Cody began to sweat – his fears from the war were coming back. He wanted to avoid shooting this man, he didn't even know if he could. In fact he was bluffing, and that realization gnawed at his soul. He was a fraud, and this Emmet could see right through him. The deputy was vaguely aware of a rifle being cocked. His eyes darted back and forth before he realized it was Hank, leveling the Henry at the other men.

Slowly, achingly slow, Emmet placed his right hand back on his reins. 'You heard him boys, let's be on our way.' His eyes never left Cody's as he walked his mount past him. The others followed him, reluctantly at first. Cody kept his Dragoon trained on them, moving the gelding so he could watch the five riders go. When they were out of range Cody re-holstered his Dragoon, his hand slick with sweat. He grabbed the reins to keep his hand from shaking. 'Let's git,' he told Hank, and whirled his horse around. His bluff had worked, but he knew deep in his bones that he wasn't yet ready to face men of violence. And that realization haunted him. He was supposed to be Cody the deputy sheriff, but in reality he was just Cody the coward.

Lionel watched the scene unfold below him. He was a good mile and a half behind the deputy and his partner, standing on a ridge, but with his spyglass he could see them talking to five other men. The situation was tense. Guns were pulled by the deputy and his friend, but no shots fired. Then the five riders rode away peacefully. That was the end of it, he thought, until he saw the riders stop, a short distance away, and mill about. They were closer to the ridge, so the gambler ducked down. A decision must have been reached, since they turned around and went back the way they came, toward the deputy. So, Lionel thought, they're going to fight after all. Good, he could be rid of the Gold Hill lawman without having to get his hands dirty. If they survived the encounter, he could come in and finish them off.

Cody urged his gelding into a canter; he wanted to make some distance in case those drifters came back. He heard Hank give a shout from behind, and half-turning in his saddle he saw Emmet and his men were coming after them hard. Cody bore down over his gelding, digging his heels into its flanks and pulling it in another direction. He could hear shots being fired. Cody didn't want to exhaust his horse, but there were too many of them to fight in the open. The deputy needed cover and fast, as the drifters were gaining ground. He dared a glance back to see if Hank was still with him, and spied him off to his left. 'Hank!' he yelled. 'Find cover!'

'Where?' Hank looked around. He was right, the area they were in now had a dearth of small hillocks or places to hide. Then he saw a small grove of ponderosa pines and oak trees off to the east. 'This way,' he pointed to the grove and kicked his gelding into a gallop. Their pursuers must have predicted their path since they also turned toward the trees at a sharp angle. Just a little bit of cover, thought Cody, and maybe I can pull the trigger. Looking a man in the eyes and then shooting him was a damned hard thing to do, but shooting from behind trees might be easier. At least he hoped. Cody and Hank made it to the tree cover first. Facing the riders Hank had the Henry ready.

'What are you waiting for, fire!' Cody barked.

With no hesitation Hank fired the Henry right into the charging men. They scattered, but not before one of them had gone down. Cody held his Dragoon in his hand, watching Hank. Then he realized that he should do something too. Without thinking he drew his gun and fired randomly – the first time he had fired a gun in anger, or rather fear, since the war. His shot was wide, and the four remaining riders were regrouping. It was lucky, thought Cody, that these men weren't professionals. They were disorganized, and their gun discipline was lacking. Their aim was off, their flanks exposed, and every time the Henry roared they fled, only to regroup a short time later. Hank had dropped another rider, so now the fight was almost even, three against two.

Of the two men shot by Hank, one was still writhing on the ground, the other looked stone cold dead. The last three riders were regrouping, but Cody could see a familiar emotion ripple across their faces – fear. None of them had a long gun, and Hank was deadly with the

Henry, keeping them off balance. Cody felt guilty, since it was supposed to be his gun, but Hank had taken it from his saddle scabbard and didn't relinquish it. In a way he was grateful that it was Hank using the rifle and not him. Cody took aim again with the Dragoon as the three remaining riders charged their position. He plunked one right on the shoulder, causing him to lose his grip. His horse bucked and the man went flying. That was it for the other two: Emmet and his remaining mounted partner wheeled their horses and rode to distance. Cody and Hank each fired a shot for good measure at the fleeing men, who were already out of range.

'Nice shooting, Hank. Your leg OK?'

'Yeah, I'm all right, it still hurts but I'll manage. I'm almost out of bullets though.'

Cody nodded, 'Let's see if these boys carried any spares in their saddlebags.' The deputy and his partner checked the three men. One was dead, and one was on the way. The man Cody shot was wounded but looked like he would live.

'What's your name?' The deputy asked him after they had bound his hands and retrieved the horses.

'I ain't telling you, squat lawman.'

Cody sadly shook his head, 'You should have listened to me when I said I wasn't after you. Whatever you did I hope it was worth it. Now two of your compadres are dead and you're all shot up. I don't have time to take you in, so you better hope your other friends come back for you.' He got back on his horse. 'We'll take your gun and the bullets. But here, you can have water and

99

this to cut yourself free in time.' He tossed the man a canteen and a knife. 'After I'm done with my business I'll come back this way. If I see you or your friends again I'll put you in the ground.' It was tough talk, Cody knew. He had shot someone for the first time since he had fled the army, but he was secretly relieved to know that the man would live.

'Did you get enough ammo?' Cody asked Hank as the two rode away from the small battlefield next to the grove.

'Humm, I found some bullets for a Sharpe's but nothing for the Henry.'

'I have spares, but not a whole lot. Better not use it unless we absolutely have to.'

'Here, you can have it back, sorry I took it.'

'That's all right, you were being smart and covering me, I'd do the same for you,' said Cody. He hoped he would, anyway. As he rode he looked down at his hand: it was shaking less, and there was less sweat on his palm. The first shooting is always the hardest, he thought. The deputy tossed the man's gun to the ground – he didn't want to be tempted to use it. They had taken the two dead men's horses, one each tied to their respective horses, to spell their mounts and give them some rest. Cody hoped in this way they could catch up to the Confederates.

When Lionel came across the scene of the shoot-out he let out a low whistle. Two men lay dead, one other lay wounded, his two friends helping him with a shoulder wound. One man jumped up and pulled his gun.

'Easy friend, I'm here to help. What happened here?'

'We ran into a lawman and his deputy.'

'Ian, shut yer mouth.'

'But Emmet, he . . . I. . . .'

'It's quite all right, I'm no fan of the law myself. Lionel Hewitt, gambler extraordinaire, looking for fame and fortune. Well, mostly fortune. May I be of assistance?' He got off the claybank and approached the wounded man. He produced a dry cloth and helped bandage the wound. 'The bullet is out?'

'Yup, dug it out meself. Robbie's a tough one'

'Good, he looks a bit woozy. Here, give him a pull of this.' He proffered a canteen of whiskey. The wounded man, Robbie, took a long swallow and then lay back down on the grass. 'Let him rest, he'll be fine. My name's Emmet, much obliged for the help.'

Lionel nodded and said, 'What officer of the law did this to you?'

Emmet scratched his head. 'He didn't say his name, but he called his partner Hank. We figured he was gonna track us down. We don't want no attention from the law, if you know what I mean.'

'Indeed I do, my friend Emmet, indeed I do. Now, what will you do about this lawdog? Surely he will track you down. Firing on a lawman is a hanging offense.'

'He's got a rifle. We can't get the drop on him.'

'Ah, but with me by your side I think we can. Is your friend well enough to travel?'

'Well, we can drag him along, or leave him behind if he's a liability. It don't matter.'

'And the bodies of your other compatriots?'

Emmet sniffed, 'Leave 'em for the coyotes.'

'A hard man, I like that. Come, we have a lawman to kill.'

CHAPTER 15

Cody looked aghast at the carnage they had come across. Bodies were strewn all over the plain – he counted fifteen then couldn't bear to look any more. Hank took a closer examination. 'It don't look like the bandits we're chasing. No sign of a wagon either,' he reported. 'I don't see any arrows either, so it wasn't Indians.'

Cody crouched down in the grass, his stomach churning, his face in his hands. Then he heard what he dreaded from Hank. 'Ah, geez, I know this one, it's Ernie, one of the miners . . . Cody, this is. . . .'

'I know,' he said, his voice far away. He had known with a quiet certainty when he had first seen the battle-field, that Talbott's posse had caught up with the Confederates. Exactly how, he wasn't sure. He wondered if Talbott was among the dead. The deputy stood up and kicked at a blade of grass. This was exactly the scenario he had wanted to avoid. The foolhardy and impatient mining baron had rushed into danger without understanding his foe, and had met disaster.

More deaths, needless, and these ones were on his head: he could have prevented this if he had got to the outlaws first.

'You think it was the same gang?' Hank said.

'I know it was.'

'What now?'

'Find them and bring 'em to justice.'

It was almost dark; they had traveled far since their shoot-out with the drifters, two days ago. Cody decided they should stop nearby and make camp. He had got over his self pity enough to move himself to some action. He owed these men, men from Gold Hill, a proper send-off. Hank rested his leg while Cody dragged the fifteen bodies into a line. It was grueling and gruesome work. The bodies had been exposed for at least a day perhaps more. Talbott wasn't among the dead, but Cody recognized a few of the faces, even twisted in their death masks, from his short time in the mining camp. Exhausted, he lay down in his bedding next to Hank in the twilight.

'What do you think happened?' said Hank.

'The posse must have gotten ahead of us when we were at the farm to fix your leg. Maybe they got better at tracking and found the wagon ruts. In any case it looks like they got the worst of it in this engagement.'

'It looked pretty even. I counted eight men from the posse, the other seven from the bandits. You still think it was the Confederates we're trailing?'

'Who else would it be?'

'There are lots of roving bands of drifters around here. Like the fellas we ran into the other day.'

Cody sighed and rubbed his eyes. 'Yeah, I suppose. It could be anybody, but I don't think the posse would get involved in a prolonged fight with anybody but them that stole the wagon.'

'You're probably right, Cody. You think we'll catch 'em?'

'We will.'

Hank was soon snoring. Cody stared up at the stars – his doubts were still there under the surface. When he had first seen the bodies his initial instinct had been to flee. He had thought that with the firefight with the drifters he had banished these feelings, but now it seemed he still had more fears to conquer. The deputy only hoped he could do so before he met with the Confederates. He would allow fear to be replaced by anger. I'll have to do it, he thought, I have no other choice.

The next morning Cody and Hank said a few words over the bodies. They lacked the tools and time for a burial so Cody placed makeshift crosses, in reality sticks tied together, on each of the bodies, even the bandits. When done, the deputy nodded to Hank. 'We're running out of time, Hank, and these Confederates are ruthless. We have to get the army involved.'

Hank let out a breath. 'I reckon we're in New Mexico Territory now. Fort Union has to be close, near Santa Fe.'

'That's good. One of us should go to the fort and tell them about these Confederate bandits. I'm a little compromised since I deserted the battlefield. That leaves you.'

'Sure, I can go Cody. I hope they believe a Texan.'

'That's your job, Hank, to convince them, if you want your gold back.'

'Good incentive Cody. What about you?'

'I'll go on following them in case they change direction. I figure they're still heading for Fort Bliss, so if you can persuade the army to help us, you can take them there to head off the Confederates.'

'Good luck, Cody.'

'Good luck, Hank, and God speed.'

Lionel and his two new friends found the field of battle just the way Cody and Hank had left it.

'Looks like someone was here, put out the bodies all nice and neat like,' said Emmet, stating the obvious.

The gambler bit back the sharp retort on his tongue, instead saying 'It looks like our quarry, the lawman, is the sentimental type.'

Ian, further ahead, was examining the ground. 'There's fresh tracks and spoor here. Two riders, riding together here, then they split into different directions, one going southeast and the other southwest.'

'Clever ruse, or spooked by the battle. We may have to split our forces as well.' Now the gambler regretted leaving Robbie behind. The third surviving member of their makeshift band had stayed to tend his wound and was then going to strike out on his own. Lionel had thought the decision was good at the time – no need to have a crippled man slowing them down – but in the light of this new development he wished they had the fourth man so they could split into two even pairs. Too

106

late now, he would have to make do.

'Emmet, you and Ian follow the southwest trail, and I'll follow the southeast trail. You know what our mark looks like. If you come across one or the other, put an end to him. We can meet back here in one week. You can have your revenge.'

The two men looked at Lionel, their faces hard masks. 'Listen, gambler man, this is becoming more trouble than it's worth. These two are hightailing it out of this territory, far away from us. Maybe Robbie had the right idea. Revenge ain't worth it.'

Lionel hesitated, mulling his options. He could dust them now, or let them leave. It was tempting to shoot this dimwitted pair, but for now he needed Emmet and Ian.

'Did I mention there's a reward? Five hundred dollars for the deputy or his partner.'

That got their attention. 'Who's paying?' Emmet asked, his eyes narrow.

'I am. Meet back here in five days with one or the other of them, dead or alive, and I'll pay you five hundred dollars.'

'Each.'

A thin smile formed on Lionel's face. 'Agreed, each. But I must have evidence, the body preferably, dead or alive. Now go, time is running out.' Lionel expected he would never see the two again. If they did succeed in killing the deputy or his Texan friend, then all the better, but they were only meant to keep the lawman and his friend busy to prevent them from reaching the Confederates or the Union Army in the region. That is, if all went according to plan.

In a week he'd be swimming in gold. If he ever did see the drifters again he was confident he could outdraw them. He smiled. 'All right, get on it, and you'll have your reward.' The drifters swung their horses for the southeast. Lionel had deliberately given them that route. He wasn't sure who they would be following, but it would keep them away from Julius and the gold wagon.

The less they knew about that the better. They hadn't asked questions, such as where Lionel would get that kind of money, or why he wanted the deputy dead. Nope, they were simple men driven by simple needs – greed, he thought. Makes my job easier. Now all he had to do was kill the lone rider headed toward the gold wagon, and meet up with Julius and Jeffrey at Fort Bliss. He would collect his reward and leave something for Julius. He patted his Navy Remington.

The landscape changed, the grasslands becoming more barren, mountainous, the sun becoming more unbearable. Cody hardly noticed, he pushed his gelding onward. Every few hours he switched it with the roan he had taken from the dead drifter. He was lucky in that the route he had chosen had several creeks and streams along it. Enough to keep the horses watered, enough to keep them going. He was deep in New Mexico Territory, so he needed to make up ground fast. His previous uncertainty was gone. Witnessing the aftermath of the shoot-out had steeled his resolve. The deputy had a grim look on his face, his eyes ahead on the road, when he heard the crack of a rifle. He reined up and dived off the roan, and rolled into a crouch; he was in a small hollow, and there was a small hill on the east side, and it was from there that the shot came. Almost immediately a rider came out from behind the hill, holding a rifle. Another rider soon followed him. Cody raised his hands.

'I'm Cody Black, deputy sheriff from Gold Hill, Colorado Territory,' he said in a loud voice.

The two horsemen rode closer and then one broke into a smile. 'Hey, Mr Talbott, it's him, the deputy.'

Cody breathed a heavy sigh. The posse, or what remained of it, had found him. Soon, more men followed. Cody cursed himself at his carelessness. The hill to the east provided a perfect ambush, and he had been too focused on tracking the wagon with the gold to notice. Looking up, Cody saw the tall form of the mining baron from Gold Hill approach him.

'Well, well, Deputy Black. You have the most impeccable timing. Always showing up after our firefights. I assume you saw our little battlefield?'

'I did, Mr Talbott. I'm sorry for your losses, really I am.'

'Not as sorry as me. I'm down to six men now, and the rest scattered to the wind. Wasn't worth their lives, apparently. A sentiment I am tending to agree with.'

'It's not worth any more lives. I told you I'll get your wagon back, and I'll do just that. You and your men need to return to Gold Hill.'

'You'll get my wagon? Well, where is it?'

'I'm working on it. You know what kind of men

you're facing, and where they are going, don't you?'

'We assumed they were heading to Mexico.'

'They are, but this is bigger than just stealing gold. These men are Confederates, and they're gonna use this gold to buy Mexican or French troops to fight the Union.'

Talbott stood up straighter on his horse, giving Cody a sharp look. 'How do you know this?'

'Just my gut feeling. I fought against men like these in the war.'

Talbott nodded, and then said 'Where's Grimes, Hank Grimes? Wasn't he with you?'

'I sent him on to the nearest Union fort. We need the army's help now.'

'If that's true, then you will need our help.'

'No. Already you've met these men twice and already you've gotten the worst of it. No, I need these men to go back to Gold Hill and trust that I will return the stolen gold, all of it. Leave this to the professionals.'

Cody regretted his last words as Talbott had a fierce look on his face. 'Why, you jumped up little mule driver. If it weren't for me you'd be starving in the mountains still. I made you deputy sheriff.'

'You sure did, and now by right of law, I am the professional, and you're just a private citizen.'

Talbott fumed and raged, spluttering out insults. Cody watched him, his hands folded in front of him, his face neutral, until Talbott ran out of steam. 'Just find my gold,' he turned his horse around. 'Come on, boys.'

Cody watched in quiet satisfaction as he saw the direction they were headed: north. Back to Gold Hill, presumably, and away from the deadly Confederates. Now, free of interference, Cody had to deliver on his promise. Cody got back on the roan and headed southeast again, for what he hoped would be the final confrontation with the Confederate bandits.

CHAPTER 16

Eventually Cody came to a small town, the Stars and Bars was flying overhead. He dropped the reins of the drifter's roan. He was riding the gelding, and it was time for him to leave the borrowed horse; someone would pick her up. The deputy knew he had to be extremely careful now: this close to Fort Bliss, or Texas itself, Confederate sympathies were high.

He left the roan on a trail leading to the town of no name, the only clue to its identity the Confederate flag fluttering softly in the breeze on top of one of the buildings, and rode around to the far side where he hoped the livery was. He took a wide arc, keeping a few miles away. Satisfied that he hadn't been spotted, he found a small grove of trees – the perfect place to wait until it was dark. It was already midday so he had time. He let the gelding loose to graze, hoping it could find water. His trail vitals were long gone, and it had been a whole day since he last ate. But the Conestoga was here, he was sure of it.

Night came and Cody checked his Henry. The deputy was thankful that Hank had returned it. The long gun would be useful, if he could see his targets. He steeled his resolve. This was a messy business, and he worried he wouldn't have the will to see it through. He remembered the images of the dead posse. Men he could have, should have, saved. No more will die, he would see to that.

Cody crept toward the town. He needed to find the wagon fast, get the team hooked up and ride it away. His hope was to drive the wagon as far away as possible, hide it, in case the army never came. It was a good plan, Cody thought, at least it was the best he could do on his own. Even if he died in the attempt it was a good way to go down, and he'd purge the cowardice from his soul forever. He was almost to the town, there were no lights, and no noise coming from the buildings. He counted less than a dozen structures, small, perhaps abandoned, and now occupied by the Confederates.

On the outskirts of town now, he could see the outline of the buildings. The wagon would be in a barn, most likely near the stables. He listened to the wind, then he heard ever so softly the telltale click of a rifle hammer being pulled back. Instinct drove him to the ground a split second before the shot sailed over his head. He pumped the Henry and from his knees fired in the direction the shot came from. The noise was sure to wake the town. His plan was in ruins.

'Hello, deputy,' a familiar voice drifted over the wind. 'You should be more careful about covering your back trail. And leaving the roan you stole from those drifters? Might as well leave me a note telling me where you are. Now it's time to die.'

Another shot was fired, followed by three more. It was all Cody could do to keep from being hit. He squirmed and rolled, moving left and right, hoping the gambler couldn't get a good read on him in the dark. Cody held his breath and waited for the sixth shot. It didn't come. Then he heard feet running, the gambler was trying to get close to him. One chance, he stood up and fired the Henry. The shot clipped the figure running toward him, dropping the gambler to the ground. The shaking he expected in his hands didn't come. Right then he didn't take time to dwell on that accomplishment. The town was stirring, lanterns were being lit, and men were shouting. They would come to investigate the shots. Throwing caution to the wind, he ran to the grove where the gelding was. Get clear of the Confederates and try again, he thought.

Once mounted he pushed the gelding into a gallop and kept it going until he couldn't hear any sounds of pursuit. Out of immediate danger now he beat his Stetson against his leg. He should have been more careful. Too careless, the deputy had forgotten about the gambler following them. It had been too many days in the past. No excuse, he would have to try again. Now, though, the Confederates would be wary and waiting for him. He'd have to be doubly careful the next time – but he couldn't give up. The wagon must be stopped, and he believed that he was the only one who could do it.

*

Hank rode at an easy pace after he and Cody parted ways. His leg still throbbed, but it was bearable. The Texan was familiar with this terrain, having come this way to get to Gold Hill. But he wasn't completely sure where the Union fort was, or if there would be any soldiers there. And even if he found the fort, there was no guarantee that the army would believe him about the stolen gold. But he had promised Cody. Besides which, any chance, even a small one, that could see his own stake recovered was worth a try.

Before too long Hank had an uneasy feeling that he was being followed. He couldn't hear anything, but the hackles on the back of his neck were standing up. Then he pinpointed it: he could hear no sound at all. No birds, not even the wind. He stopped his horse and sat up in the saddle, peering around. The Texan saw that he had wandered into a small glen, a good ambush site. He reached for his Colt and his movement caused the horse to continue walking. A split second later a lead slug hit his mount's rump. The horse bucked hard at the pain, which threw Hank to the ground, and ran off. Another shot echoed through the glen, so Hank made for cover. Two shots rang out simultaneously: two shooters, at least.

Hank had his Colt out. He fired at random, hoping to keep his opponents off balance. Instead, he received return fire, forcing him to dive behind a small boulder. That was stupid of me, he thought, now I'm pinned down. He wished he hadn't given Cody back the Henry, it would be nice to have it now. He checked his ammo. He had five shots left in his Colt and another fifteen bullets as spares – more than enough. He paused, listening for the shot, chambering another round into his six shooter. He counted to five, and when no shots came, he let out a slow long breath. He heard rustling in the bushes. The shooters were trying to surround him. Trying to head them off, the Texan stood up and began firing in a circle, emptying his Colt. Without pause he ran straight ahead. His ploy worked, his pursuers were now behind him. Bullets ricocheted near his feet.

He tried to chamber his rounds while he ran, but only managed to get in two before he stumbled over a rock and fell, his wounded leg letting him down. Cursing, the Texan's left arm sprawled out, while his right arm remained tucked underneath his body, his right hand wrapped tightly around his Colt as he hit the ground hard. He gasped for breath and heard footsteps running from behind. It was too late to hide – Hank just hoped he could get off a clean shot.

The footsteps stopped. He could hear heavy breathing. The prospector decided to play dead.

'Did we get him, Emmet?'

'Not sure, maybe we ought to pump another couple of bullets in him just in case, Ian. Aim for the leg, wound him a bit.'

'He's wanted dead or alive by that gambler.'

'Yeah, but do you want to drag a dead body all the way back? They stink to high heaven. We just wound him a little, that way we know he ain't going nowhere and it'll be easy.'

'Yeah, you're right Emmet.'

'Of course I'm right, now shoot him in the leg.'

At that moment Hank rolled over, bringing up his Colt: rolling from left to right he fired at the two men standing not three feet away from him. His first bullet slammed into the chest of the surprised Emmet, whose lifeless body crumpled, his facial expression one of complete surprise. The second bullet hit Ian in the right shoulder, and the drifter stumbled backwards. Hank scrambled to his knees, loading his Colt. He got three bullets chambered and fired two shots at the staggering man. Ian fell over, his body twitched and then was still. Only then did Hank take a breath.

He reloaded his Colt in case there were more men coming for him. Six chambered and four spares: ten bullets. Hank thought it was bad luck to use a dead man's gun, but it was still two or three days' travel to the fort. Better to have the extras just in case. He took Emmett's and Ian's guns, though their caliber were not a match to his own. He started to look for a horse. He tested his bum leg, still throbbing in pain, and gingerly walked on it. He couldn't let it slow him down.

The Texan found the drifters' horses grazing in a nearby glen. His own horse had joined them. Hank thought long and hard about taking the extra horses, but ultimately decided against it. Their presence might bring too many unwanted questions from the Union army. Horse thieves were hanged, and one man riding with three horses might mark him as a horse thief.

117

Besides, taking the guns was bad enough. Hank mounted his horse and rode on south. He had a notion now of what to tell the army commanders to convince them to come. He only hoped they would believe him.

CHAPTER 17

Lionel awoke with a splitting headache. He was lying on a bed in a small shack. Sitting up, he saw a mug with water on a stool next to the bed. He took a sip, then lay back down, wondering how long it would be before the inevitable confrontation with Julius and Jeffrey. He wasn't waiting long when the door slammed open. In walked Julius, his face a furious thundercloud. Jeffrey trailed after him, looking concerned. Three other men, all armed with rifles, followed them in. The last man in shut the door. Lionel looked at Julius, trying to hold the man's hard stare. In the end, he couldn't. After a long time Julius spoke.

'You assured me, gambler, you would take care of that deputy. That you would watch our back trail. What in tarnation happened?'

Lionel couldn't help swallowing. 'I underestimated him. The deputy was more resourceful and resilient than I thought. It won't happen again.'

'Damn right it won't Hewitt. I ought to string you up right now for endangering my men's lives. Jeffrey here acted as your lone advocate, for which I have admonished him. Instead of stringing you up I'm giving you one day's head start. If we ever cross paths again I'll kill you. Consider this the end of our partnership. Jeffrey here will see to your recompense.' The Confederate leader stormed out of the hut, followed by his men, leaving Lionel alone with Jeffrey. The Confederates' second-in-command gave Lionel a sympathetic look, then sat down on the stool, removing the water mug.

'I'm sorry about Julius. It was all I could do to prevent him from killing you outright. I still feel we owe you for your help, but now you've become a liability. I agree with Julius that if we ever see you again, we'll kill you.'

'Seems fair,' Lionel said.

Jeffrey counted out gold coins from a bag and then handed them to the gambler. 'This is your compensation. It isn't as much as we promised, but your employment has been terminated early. Take it or leave it, that's what we're giving you. When you're ready you can leave, but be gone by sundown.' He stood up, and headed for the entrance. 'Take care, gambler,' he said before he shut the door.

Lionel sat back down on the bed, fingering the gold dollars. Damn, he thought, now I've done it. I should have killed that dang deputy when I had the chance. Well, nothing for it now. He itched to put a slug in Julius and take the rest of his gold. But it wasn't practical at this point, better to get some distance from the Confederates. He gathered his belongings and strapped on his Navy Remington. He walked out of the

120

hut, the sun blinding him, forcing him to squint. The gambler figured it was mid-afternoon, so he only had a few hours to get clear. He found his horse, waiting just outside, saddled and looking well rested. The Confederates were serious about him leaving, guess he would oblige them now. He mounted his claybank and looked around. The street was empty, his former employees gone, but Lionel had little doubt that his every move was being watched from the scattered buildings. He tipped his hat, and said 'Thank you kindly for the money. I hope I won't be seeing you any time soon.' Then he gigged his horse into a trot – no sense in showing them he was running scared – and casually left the nondescript town.

Once at a safe distance, several miles away, Lionel stopped for the night. He had no real plan now other than to get the money owed to him. Jeffrey had given him a paltry sum, only one-tenth of what he was promised. Julius had made a big show of blustering and threatening Lionel, but the card sharp was no novice, and would not be easily intimidated. It might be risky to go up against these hard men. But they were fooling with Lionel's livelihood, not to mention routinely insulting him. Lionel could be just as dangerous and just as hard as Julius, and now he aimed to prove it. Perhaps he would seek out the deputy. He had proved resourceful in the past. No, better to follow the Confederates and stay out of the way. Wait for an opportunity to strike. It was always the way he worked best, in the shadows, incognito. He'll get his gold, Lionel thought, and put that well deserved bullet into that Confederate officer's forehead. He relished the image.

Cody crouched in the tall grass as he watched the wagon move out of the small town. It had been two days since his aborted attempt to steal the wagon. He had fled that night fearing dogged pursuit, but returned when he felt he had evaded his pursuers. He was surprised to find the Confederates still here. He puzzled over why it was taking them so long to move further south. Then he saw a group of three riders approaching from the south. Soon after, the town was a beehive of activity as men packed and saddled horses and the infamous gold wagon was brought out. Scouts, Cody surmised, checking to see if the way was clear of Yankees. Now, they were ready. It wouldn't take them long to reach Fort Bliss, and Cody hoped Hank could convince the army to head them off. Cody crouched lower as the caravan rode close to him. His horse was hidden a few hundred yards away.

The Confederates passed with none looking in his direction. He was a good fifty yards away in some heavy brush. When the group had made it to the edge of his eyesight, distant specks on the horizon, he jumped up and raced back to his horse. The wagon would keep their pace slow, he only had to shadow them. The deputy had counted fifteen men, and he didn't see any sign of the gambler. Perhaps he was gone. It was no matter. He needed to focus on the fifteen Confederates and the wagon.

Cody was out of breath when he reached his horse,

122

hobbled but saddled. He mounted and rode after the Confederates. The wagon cut a wide swath through the grass, making it easy to follow. He stopped short when he saw two horsemen in the distance standing motionless along the trail. A rearguard, or more drifters. They spotted him and moved toward him. He could see now that both were holding rifles: a rearguard, and they meant to kill him. He wheeled his horse around, trying to get away. The two men rode hard after him, gaining ground.

Cody lurched off the makeshift path and rode east. Holding the reins in one hand he reached for the Henry, almost dropping it when his horse hit rough ground. He cocked the rifle and brought it to bear. Firing behind him one-handed he got a shot off. His aim was poor and the shot was off mark. But that triggered retaliation from his pursuers. They both brought their rifles up and shot at him. One whizzed past his horse's ear causing the mount to skitter. Panic welled up inside him. He was outgunned and soon those horses, faster than his own, would catch him.

The deputy veered to the left, the two Confederates were trying to flank him, box him in. He tried to aim again but he had to take both hands off the reins, causing the horse to slow. His pursuers were less than a hundred yards away: he aimed for the one coming up on his left and shot his mount out from under him. The rider flew off as the horse went down. Cody pumped a bullet into the soldier before he could gain his feet. The man groaned for a moment, then lay still.

But the deputy had made himself vulnerable to the

other rider, coming up hard on his right. He could see him out of the corner of his eye, too late to bring his gun around. The man was charging at a full gallop, his gun aimed, about to pull the trigger. Cody blinked and saw the man clutch at his back, and drop his weapon. Then he heard the crack sound of a shot: the other rearguard was down, writhing in pain. Cody put him out of his misery with a swift shot to the heart.

Someone had helped him, had taken a shot at the second man. Without that Cody would have been dead. He looked off into the distance and saw a lone figure riding a familiar horse.

The man tipped his hat, then shouted, 'Good luck, deputy!' wheeled his horse and was gone. The gambler, Lionel. He must have switched sides, or found himself on the outs. Unless it was an elaborate trap. Not likely, Cody thought. Still, better to be cautious around him – the gambler couldn't be trusted, even if he had saved his life.

The rearguard would be missed. The gold thieves would come looking for them and want to hunt down their killer. But at least that was two Confederates he wouldn't have to face again. He checked his hands: the trembling had almost stopped, though his palms were still sweaty. He'd never get used to killing, or he hoped not, but at least he knew he could do it. Shame filled him as he thought of the men he had abandoned on the battlefield. No, this will make things right. I won't be a hero, he thought, but at least I can hold my head up. But now he had to hide out again.

As he rode he relived his battle with the two rearguards. The Confederates were down to thirteen men now: if he could keep picking them off in ones and twos then he might have a chance to stop them. He needed to have a plan in case Hank couldn't make it to the fort or couldn't convince the Unionists to march. He mulled it over in his mind and thought this was better than trailing the wagon. The only trouble was baiting the Confederates to chase him in small numbers. It would be risky, but worth a shot. He would have to creep up on them real slow. Lionel could help him. No, Cody thought, better not to trust him. Cody rode in a wide circle, slowly doubling back after several hours, once he thought he wasn't being followed any more. It was after dark before he saw the dimly lit campfires of the caravan. The deputy stayed a safe distance away, chewing on dried rabbit meat from a jackrabbit he had shot a few days before. He watched and waited.

CHAPTER 18

At first Lionel was angry with himself for helping the deputy. He had needlessly exposed himself and ran the risk of being killed by Julius. However, after he had some time to think on the subject he thought it might work to his advantage. He had saved the lawman's life thus allowing him to continue fighting the Confederates. Both Confederates were dead and no one else had chanced upon him. The only person who knew it was him was the lawman, and he wasn't going to tell Julius or Jeffrey anything. Besides, he may have made a valuable ally. He had camped further north of the deputy, keeping him within sight and between the gambler and Julius. He hadn't lit a fire, neither had the deputy. Lionel had to trust that Cody was still out there watching the dwindling campfires of the Confederates. Trying to stay awake, he couldn't help nodding off. He awoke to the sound of footsteps; the dawn was just cracking over the horizon. Lionel scrambled to get his gun. He held his breath when *click*, a hammer drew back.

126

'Easy gambler, I ain't gonna kill ya. At least not yet.' The speaker came from behind him.

'Howdy deputy.'

'It was you who killed the other outrider. You saved my life.'

Lionel nodded.

'What happened? The last time we met you were fixing to put lead into me.'

'My, uh, circumstances have changed. Due to your uncanny ability to survive I have fallen from grace. My former employer has cut all ties with me.'

'So why are you still here?'

'He failed to fulfil his monetary obligation to me.'

Cody nodded, a knowing smile on his face. 'I see, so you want due compensation for failing to finish your job.'

'Well, when you put it that way, it makes it sound like I am to blame. You should count yourself fortunate that I have decided to change sides.'

'Yes, forgive me if I am not overwhelmingly gracious, considering the fact that you have tried to kill me more than once. By my reckoning you still owe me.'

Lionel shifted his body, causing the deputy to aim his Colt more closely. The gambler showed his hands and Cody relaxed. 'I'm not sure I trust you yet. I want you to know I know you're here. Stay out of my way, if you don't want trouble.'

'Duly noted.'

The deputy turned to leave and Lionel couldn't resist calling out to him. 'Cody, whether you trust me or not, we're on the same side . . . for now.' The lawman kept walking without a hitch in his step. This boy was more resourceful than he had thought – it wasn't often someone got the drop on Lionel Hewitt. Maybe he was backing the right horse after all, he thought with a smile.

Later that morning the caravan moved out. Lionel rode for higher ground he knew the wagon couldn't traverse, the better to watch over the gold. The men were spread out to either side and in front and behind the wagon, protecting it; Julius was taking no more chances. They were getting close to Fort Bliss now. Lionel remembered the plan vaguely: at some point riders from the fort would come north to meet them and help escort the gold to Mexico. Once across the border they would be safe. But Lionel didn't know when or where Julius was scheduled to meet the fort's contingent, or even if that was the plan still. Whatever the case, he knew Cody was running out of time.

He lazily watched the progress of the wagon and its outriders from the high plateau. He patted his horse, when he was shaken from his reverie by a loud gunshot. Peering into the distance he saw one of Julius's men fall over. The others scrambled in the direction of the shot. The deputy, he thought, had grown more courageous. Picking off the Confederates one at a time. Lionel smiled; as long as the fool boy didn't get himself killed he might have a chance to take back his gold. Lionel rode down off the bluff. The shot had come from the other eastward side, which was lower in elevation. He headed down toward the sound of the shot. Whether he admitted it or not, the kid needed his help.

The gambler drew rein when he saw a cloud of dust approaching. He had doubled back, guessing correctly that the lawman would be headed away from the Confederates. He was, and was coming on fast, directly at Lionel, with a horde of angry Confederates on his tail. Damnation, Lionel thought, I'll be pegged for sure. He steered his horse into a clump of trees, waiting for Cody and his pursuers to pass. No one looked in his direction: instead they kept riding. Lionel counted four riders after the deputy. His was a bold move, but reckless. The Confederates' mounts were faster than the deputy's, so Lionel waited a five count, then burst from the trees after them. He had his Navy Remington out and fired at the nearest rider. The shot went wide but had the desired effect. The rider he had shot at peeled off, and so did one of his companions. They turned around to charge right at Lionel. Well, that evens the odds a little, he thought. Now it's two on one.

They were coming at him single file. Unflinching, he dug his spurs into the ribs of his horse, firing his Remington. The lead rider, the one he had previously missed, took the shot right in the chest. The second Confederate had his gun ready but Lionel was too fast for him, gunning him down before he could even aim. Quick work, the deputy should be able to handle the other two. Now to light a shuck before more of Julius's men come and discover him.

Lionel was right, Cody did dispatch the other Confederate riders. He trotted up and saw the aftermath of the battle. Both riders lay dead, their still saddled horses grazing peacefully nearby. The deputy was sitting on his gelding looking serene with his Henry in hand.

'Thank you again for the help. I still don't trust your motives, but I'm convinced you aren't working for the rebels anymore.'

'Indeed, I am my own man once again. We have a common purpose, you and I. To prevent the gold from reaching Mexico.'

'And now there are only seven riders left.'

Lionel smiled, 'Nine if you count Julius and Jeffrey, the officers, on the wagon. But I must warn you, there will be more coming to meet them from Fort Bliss, perhaps too many for us to handle.'

'Don't worry, I sent my friend Hank to treat with the Union army, tell them what had happened. If he can convince them, they will come in force to stop the Confederates.'

Lionel cleared his throat, and shifted awkwardly in his saddle. 'Yes, well about that. You see, before my falling out with Julius and his band, I recruited a few men, drifters, that you and your friend had run into.'

Cody gave him a hard look.

'I sent them after Hank, promising them a reward. I'm sorry, but he may be dead.'

Cody stared at him for a long time, his face a dark cloud of fury. At length he said, 'How many?'

'Just two men. I'm sure your friend could handle them.'

'You better hope so, for your sake. When is this contingent going to meet the wagon?'

Lionel shrugged, 'I have no idea. I'm not even sure

if that was still in the plans or not.'

Cody nodded, 'I'm running out of ammo. I'm not sure if I can take on all ten of these men. If what you say is true, that more Confederates are coming, then I need your help to take out the group now. My plan was to bleed them in ones and twos, as I thought I had time. But if more Confederates show up, then time's running out. Besides, I'm wasting bullets with this strategy. I still don't trust you, but I could use your help.'

The gambler smiled, 'I am ready to assist you in any way I can, my good deputy.'

'If Hank doesn't come I'll assume he's dead, then I'll kill you on general principle.'

'I wouldn't have it any other way.'

'All right, let's go. They'll be ready for us now.'

'Ah, but they don't know we have teamed up. I am your secret weapon.'

'Good to know. And I'll warn you for the only time, you double-cross me and I'll put a bullet clean through you.' Cody gigged his horse and Lionel followed, keeping his smile hidden from his now partner.

CHAPTER 19

Cody breathed deep, sucking in air. He sat on his gelding fingering the Henry. He was down to just a few cartridges left for the rifle, and a handful of bullets for his Colt. The deputy didn't know how much ammo the gambler had for his Navy Remington. They faced seven Confederate soldiers and two officers, all veteran, gun-hardened men. The duo were shadowing the shrinking cavalcade from high ground and at length Cody saw the two officers emerge from the wagon, where they had been for some private meeting. One man, tall in stature, mounted a fiery black stallion and barked orders to the others. The obvious commander, Cody thought. The other man also mounted a horse and rode off at a gallop. Lionel's voice came to him in a near whisper.

'The one on the black horse there is Julius Tucker, I reckon he's a major or a colonel in the Confederate army. They never used ranks, at least not in front of me. Now, that fellow that rode off is Jeffrey Cranster, I don't know what rank he was, but he is Julius's second.'

'Where's he going?'

Lionel shrugged. 'My guess is to get to the fort to bring more reinforcements.'

'How far away is Fort Bliss?'

'Two days, maybe more, it depends on how fast the wagon travels. Ole Jeffrey will run his steed into the grave if need be. He'll reach the fort in a day or less. Figure a quick turn around and a hundred Confederates will converge on us in a day and a half.'

'Then it will be too late,' said Cody, rubbing his temple.

'Most definitely, from Fort Bliss it's just a hop, skip and a jump to the Mexican border, then it's all over.'

'All right, so now we have nine men to deal with. How much ammo do you have?'

'Enough.'

Cody gave him a slanted look, 'What in the hell is that supposed to mean? Talk straight.'

The gambler stood taller in his saddle. 'By my count you need me more than I need you. Now, I've agreed to help you in order to recover what's rightly mine, but I don't cater to being ordered about. Not by Julius, and certainly not by you, deputy. I have enough bullets for my purposes, that's all you need to know.'

Cody's face grew hot, burning under the tongue lashing. 'We need to work together,' he said at length, forcing the words through gritted teeth. 'I need to trust you in battle.'

'I understand – rest assured I will gun down those that need to be gunned.'

'All right, fair enough, but after the gold is recovered you and I will need to talk.'

The gambler smiled, a wicked smile. 'I look forward to it.'

Cody and Lionel spent the next hour formulating a plan. The Confederates were still moving south. There were six horsemen, three up front, spearheaded by Julius Tucker, and three to the rear of the wagon. The wagon had a driver and another soldier riding shotgun. The cavalcade were moving swiftly now, trying to make ground, not caring about their pursuers. The plan was for Cody to ride ahead of the riders while Lionel sniped at them from the back trail.

Their idea was full of holes, but it was the best they could come up with. The hope was that they could split the riders in two, with half attacking Cody and the other half going after the gambler. Three on one wasn't great odds, but better than eight on two. With both groups off chasing the shooters, the wagon would be left virtually unprotected. The deputy and gambler would then double back and hit the exposed wagon, killing the driver and guard, then get it clear before the mounted Confederates came back. A lot of things could go wrong, but Cody was desperate to stop the wagon before it got any closer to its ultimate destination.

The deputy spurred the gelding on, travelling out of the line of sight of the gold robbers; he didn't know how much the horse had left in him. He regretted leaving the roan behind, but it would have slowed him down too much. He leaned over and whispered into the gelding's ear. 'When this is over, big fella, I'll make sure you get as many oats as you can eat.' The horse seemed to respond and galloped all the harder. When he was about a mile ahead of the Confederates he drew rein and jumped off. There was no high ground here, the plateaus had leveled out, but the deputy spied a grouping of boulders and hid out there.

Before long the rumble of the wagon wheels could be heard approaching. He cocked the Henry and opened fire as the first rider came into view. He didn't care if he hit anyone or not. It was a bonus if he could knock off one or two of the riders, but the main point was to separate them from the wagon. The Confederates scattered at the bullet. The commander, Julius, barked an order: 'Spread out, don't leave the wagon!' Another shot came from behind – good, he thought, Lionel has joined the fray. Cody got off another shot, trying to bait them.

'Behind those rocks, shoot over there.'

Cody ate dirt while he endured a fusillade of bullets.

'Keep on them, don't let up.'

'Julius, there's someone shooting at us from the rear.'

'They're trying to separate us from the wagon. Go, keep the wagon moving. I'll deal with this scum.'

Another storm of bullets was unleashed, and Cody kept his cover. He heard the thunder of hoofbeats, and then silence.

'Come on out, lawman – or are you the gambler? I figured you two would wind up together. I bet you had this planned all along. That danged Missourian couldn't shoot for beans. Well, no matter now, you ain't getting the gold. We've got big plans for it.'

A shot hit the ground, kicking dirt into Cody's face. He had one chance now to kill the commander. In one move he jumped to his feet and aimed the Henry, pumping off a shot. He dropped the rifle and drew his Colt, but the Confederate leader had backed off, riding behind a screen of brush so Cody couldn't get a shot at him. Julius rode a distance away, trailing his men who were rapidly fading away on the horizon. Cody could hear his voice as he rode, 'Not much of a coward now, are ya lawman? Looks like we put steel in your spine. Come close to my wagon again and I'll fill you full of lead.'

Cody rushed to his horse, grabbing the Henry along the way. He was met by Lionel who rode hard to intercept him. 'Hold up, deputy,' he said, his hand held up.

'What's wrong?' Cody replied, readying the rifle just in case the gambler was turning on him.

'Our plan didn't work. They won't leave the wagon, no matter what.'

'I know that,' Cody said with a frown.

'So, what's your play?'

'Chase them down and get the wagon.'

Lionel chuckled, 'Don't be a fool, there are still too many of them. I plugged one of them. Did you get any?'

'Nope.'

'So there are still seven of them, and only two of us. You better hope your friend shows up with the cavalry.'

'No, for *your* sake, you better hope he does.'

The gambler was silent at that remark. At length he said, 'All right, we'll do it your way. We'll chase them down and gun them from behind until they're all dead. But rest the horses first, otherwise we'll be stranded.'

Cody agreed, and the two let the horses graze and rest. But after an hour, Cody began to get antsy. 'Don't worry,' said Lionel, 'We'll catch up to them. They have to rest, too.'

'What about Jeffrey and the reinforcements?'

'Hell boy, it's only been an hour. We'll find them in plenty of time. Saddle up, let's go.'

Cody mounted his gelding, hoping the horse was refreshed and gigged him to a canter, with the gambler falling in behind.

They came upon the cavalcade of Confederates after dusk. Audaciously they had lit a campfire, and the smell of cooked bacon wafted under Cody's nostrils. His stomach growled involuntarily. He had run out of trail vitals a while back, and had had to subsist on rabbits and creek water. Sheer will kept him going: he needed to see this to the end.

'They'll have guards posted,' said Lionel.

'Right, they know we're coming. But they're not scared.'

'They know their boys are coming, maybe tonight.'

'Then this is the last chance.'

The gambler nodded. Cody set his face into a mask

of grim determination. They both knew this night would be one of bloodshed. The duo was holed up a few hundred yards from the camp, where the horses were picketed for the night. Lionel drew out a long Bowie knife. 'I'm not much good with this, but we need a sure way of silencing the sentries.'

Cody drew out his skinning knife.

'Skinny, but it will do in a pinch. You know, deputy, I was aiming to lay low and see what happened with the gold. I wanted what's mine, and I still do, but I wasn't willing to confront Julius. At least not right away. Then I saw you going full guns at these hardened war veterans and I was impressed. I couldn't just let you die. Not without getting the gold recovered, at least. So you dragged me in on your side. And here I thought all this time I had you pegged as a coward. You sure proved me wrong.'

'I didn't, though. I was a coward, still am. I'm trying to do my part to make amends.'

'Thank you for the revelation, but we can discuss these philosophical matters after we recover the gold, and I get what's mine.'

'You brought it up, and you ain't getting a piece of this gold. It ain't yours.'

'We'll see, deputy – right now just take care of the sentries. Oh, and leave Julius to me. I have a score to settle. A man who sasses me gets a bullet between the eyes.'

Cody didn't respond, preparing his mind for what he had to do. He'd bayonetted men before, in the war, but had never assassinated someone with a knife. It felt like dirty work, but he swallowed his disgust. It was necessary. As one, and without words, the two men crept through the darkness toward the camp, knives gleaming in the moonlight, and a grim, determined look on their faces.

CHAPTER 20

There were two sentries on the north-east side of the camp where Cody and Lionel were creeping toward the camp. The Confederates had let the fire burn low so their night vision could focus. Lionel took the first one down, and Cody marveled at his blinding speed. He broke through the brush right as the man turned his back, his hand coming over his mouth as his Bowie slid across his mark's throat. The man didn't even whimper as he collapsed and bled out. The sight shocked Cody, and unwanted memories began to flood back to him.

'Cody, snap out of it. Get the other one now.' Cody shook himself out of his apprehensions and did what he was bid. He was OK with a gun now, or at least he hoped he still was, shooting a man at some distance, but knife work was tough, too intimate. You can hear the man breathe before his life is sucked from him. With that thought stalking him he crawled through the grass, until he was almost on top of the other sentry. He had his knife out, but before the sentry walked near his position he grabbed a big rock. The deputy held his breath. When the sentry turned in another direction he leapt to his feet and brought the rock down hard on the back of the man's head. He watched the sentry crumple and fall without a sound.

'Different method than I expected,' Lionel said as he sidled up to Cody.

'It worked, didn't it?'

'There are two more sentries on the far side of the camp. Hey, this is easy, we should have done this a long time ago.'

They heard rustling in the brush, then a gruff voice called out, 'Clem? Jeb? Report in all clear.' Then there was the sound of a rifle being cocked, and two men came charging toward Cody and Lionel, one carrying a Sharps.

'So much for easy,' said Cody, diving for cover as the Sharps rifle boomed. That report woke the camp. Another sentry discovered the bodies of Clem and Jeb and shouted 'Ambush!' Cody heard Julius's loud voice bark an order, and four more men were running toward him. 'Fan the breeze, deputy. They've got us outgunned.' Lionel had moved deeper into the brush, heading toward a grove of juniper trees. The two snipers had waited for their fellows, then the six men closed ranks. All were holding rifles and had Colt or Smith & Wesson side arms. Cody scrambled backwards. The men were distracted by the noise Lionel was making in his headlong dash for the juniper grove, so Cody stayed down. There was no way he could compete against that firepower. Then there was the crack of a whip and a 'hey ya!', signaling the wagon was moving

141

out. It looked like Julius wasn't taking any chances and had harnessed the team post haste.

The noise was an additional distraction, and Cody took the opportunity to gain his feet. He ran in the opposite direction of the gambler, hoping the Confederates' attention would be drawn the other way. Sorry Lionel, he thought, but the wagon is more important. A bandit turned around and fired in his direction, the bullet chipping a nearby tree. Cody's lungs burned as he burst into the makeshift camp. Sure enough, the wagon was gone, but he spied a line of horses picketed nearby with saddles lying next to them. He grabbed the mane of one horse, already agitated by the gunshots, untied it and mounted it bareback. The horse nearly bucked off the strange rider, but Cody dug his heels into its flanks, and the wild horse bounded away after the wagon.

The horse he had chosen was fast, and Cody just managed to keep on, steering by the mane and with his knees. He was lucky, Julius had slowed ahead. Fifty yards from the wagon he jumped off the lively bronco, landing hard on his shoulder. He stood up, wincing, but there was the wagon dead ahead. He ran and leaped on to the back, grabbing hold of the sides, and hauled himself over the edge. Once inside he struck a match, and his eyes lit up as he saw bags and chests filled with gold, nuggets and dust. There was more gold here than he'd ever seen in his life. He reckoned no one, other than some kings in Europe, had ever seen so much gold. Recovering from his initial surprise, Cody doused the match, drew his Colt, and started toward

142

the front where Julius was driving the team.

The wagon lurched, and Cody lost his footing. Then it came to a full stop. He heard Julius shout out, then the cacophonous sound of hundreds of hoofs thundering together. A sinking feeling grew in his stomach – the reinforcements from Fort Bliss had arrived.

Cody stayed hidden in the wagon, covering himself with bags of gold. He was certain that Julius didn't know he was in the wagon, so as long as no one looked inside he should be safe. Loud voices came to him as the Confederates milled about their leader.

'Good work, Jeffrey, got here just in time. That damned deputy's been dogging our trail. I think the gambler teamed up with him, or he has another partner.'

'Where are the rest of the men?'

'Tracking down the deputy. I pulled the wagon out here to keep it safe and see if we can rendezvous. How many did you bring?'

'Colonel Tucker, sir,' a third voice said in a heavy Texan drawl. 'I'm Major Stallworth with the 5th Cavalry, 2nd Regiment under General Sibley, sir. I bring a hundred mounted men, sir.'

'Excellent. Major, this gold shipment needs to be escorted all the way to the Mexican border. Think you can handle that?'

'Sir, yes sir.'

'Outstanding. Let's wait for the others. At first light we'll move out, regardless if they catch up to us.'

Cody felt his heart pound: he was alone, surrounded

by a hundred or more Confederates who would kill him at first sight. He buried himself deeper under the bags of gold. Considering his options, he knew he didn't have many. All he could do was hunker down and wait for an opportunity to steal the wagon, if one ever came. Tired from the late night, Cody couldn't help himself from drifting off into sleep.

When he awoke he heard more voices and felt the wagon lurch into motion. The first light of dawn shone through the flaps. Cody rubbed his eyes, sat up, and peered at the buckboard. Someone else, shorter than Julius, was driving the wagon. Another man was riding shotgun.

'Everyone make it back?' the driver asked.

'Jeb and Zeke didn't, and Clem got a nasty welt on his head.'

'Dang, did they catch the fellers?'

The shotgun man scratched his face, 'Nope, neither of them.'

'Oh well, they won't bother us none now.'

'Yeah, too many for them to handle.' The conversation drifted in another direction, talking about women and whiskey, and Cody tuned it out. So Lionel had survived. He wondered if the gambler was still gunning for the gold, or the deputy, after Cody had abandoned him. No, that wasn't fair, thought Cody: Lionel had been the first to run. He put him out of his mind. The wagon rode on, the press of horsemen protecting it, with Cody stuck right in the middle.

It was daylight now, and Cody was about to do something drastic: burn the wagon. He had a few matches

144

left, and though it was a risky gamble, he decided this was his only choice. In the confusion he could slip away, and like this he would halt the wagon's progress. The deputy was steeling his nerves, working up the courage, when the clarion call of a cavalry charge sounded. At first he thought it was more Confederates, but the men around the wagon milled about in confusion. The driver halted the wagon, and the shotgun man stood up.

'What is it?' he asked an unseen person.

'It's the Yankees! Colonel Tucker and the Major want us in battle lines, keep the wagon moving. It needs to get to Fort Bliss no matter what.'

Cody couldn't believe his luck. Hank had done it, he had brought the army! Now it was two on one. The lawman waited while the wagon continued to move, screened no doubt by the line of Confederate cavalry as they met the charge of the Union forces. He counted to twenty and then, thinking they were clear of the main body of troops, he stealthily crawled to the front. Once in range he kicked the man riding shotgun hard, causing him to fall over and under the wagon. He whipped out his Dragoon and aimed it at the driver: 'Get off!' The driver didn't have to be told twice. He dropped the reins and jumped to the ground. Cody grabbed the reins before the team could slow, and urged them on. He changed direction, heading away from the fort. He could hear the shots and shouts from the battle, and hoped he had enough time to hide the wagon, or at least the gold.

CHAPTER 21

Lionel watched the battle unfold from a distance. He had run like hell when Cody had abandoned him to take off after the wagon – with six men after him he had no choice. It wasn't easy to lose his pursuers, but the darkness of night kept them from getting a bead on him and he managed to reach his horse. As he rode off he took a potshot at one, and the shot was lucky, hitting his pursuer. Although he had ridden off he came back to shadow the wagon. He almost cried in despair when he saw the cavalry company arrive, but now it looked as if Cody's gambit had paid off: his friend had brought the Union army, and now the gold was exposed, and isolated. He circled wide, avoiding the battle, and keeping the wagon in sight.

He was mildly surprised to see first one man, then another jump, or fall, from the conveyance. Then the wagon abruptly changed direction. The deputy, Lionel surmised, thinking that boy has nine lives. Ah, but his ninth life was about to be used up. He spurred his horse. In the process he ran down one of the wagon

riders. He then shot the other one as he tried to flee.
No sense in having any witnesses. Now, with the rest of
the Confederates occupied, he could take the wagon at
his leisure. Riding at a canter he soon caught up to it.

'My thanks, deputy, for securing my gold. I think I
will take it from here.'

The lawman reined in the team and stood on the
buckboard facing Lionel, his Dragoon in hand. 'Like
hell you will. This gold don't belong to you.'

'I was willing to spare your life considering the help
you've given, but now you are fast becoming an irritant.
Just for abandoning me at the camp I should plug you.
Now get down off that wagon.'

Lionel's hand slipped to his Navy Remington: he still
had six shots in it. He thought he could beat Cody on
the draw, even with the Colt already in the deputy's
hand. But their delay had not gone unnoticed. The
battle had shifted, and some Confederates were being
thrown back in their direction.

'Hell fire and damnation,' Lionel said as he saw a
troop riding toward them. But when he saw who led
them a smile crept on his face. 'Jeffrey, my good man.
Nice to see you again.'

'Lionel, so you were the one helping the lawman.
Julius was right. Now you're going to die.'

'As promised?'

The Confederate only nodded grimly. There were six
men with him, all looking weary from the fighting.
Lionel half turned and quickly drew his Remington,
emptying two saddles. Cody had followed suit, firing his
Dragoon from the wagon. Another Confederate was

down before the rest, including Jeffrey, scrambled for cover.

'We make a good team, deputy, shame I'm gonna have to kill ya soon.'

'We'll see, Lionel. Just now I'm more worried about these Confederates.'

'Nothing to worry about. Jeffrey? Can you hear me? If you see Julius tell him I've got a bullet with his name on it. It's going right between his eyes.' Lionel rode in a circle around the wagon, making sure the Confederates weren't trying to sneak behind him.

'Not likely, Hewitt. Once the colonel takes care of that ragtag bunch of Yankees he'll gun you or see you swing. Either way, I'll enjoy the show. Shame, Lionel, I was one of your defenders. I gave you plenty of chances and in the end you betray me. Hell, I'll gun you myself.'

The Confederate officer had talked too much for too long. Distracted, focused on Lionel, he hadn't noticed how close the deputy had got to his position. Cody was stealthy, coming in from behind, while Lionel sat his horse, a hundred paces away, in front of the grove of trees the Confederates had found shelter in. Just as Cody was getting close, Lionel charged his claybank, firing his reloaded Navy Remington. Cody took the cue and rushed the trailing Confederates, shooting one off his horse, and another one's horse out from under him. So bunched together were they that the wounded animal careened into the other riders, managing to knock Jeffrey off balance and off his horse. Lionel smiled as he took out the last two soldiers, leaving the officer alone, unarmed and unhorsed.

'My, my, how the tables have turned. Still going to enjoy the show, Jeffrey?' The Confederate officer gave him a sullen look. He was on his knees where he had fallen from his horse, his hand straying toward his weapon lying nearby.

'Hold on, Lionel. Give him a chance to surrender. He can be a prisoner of war.' Cody was standing next to the fallen Confederate, helping him to his feet; but watching the scene, Lionel grew angry.

'I'm not fighting a war. In fact, I'm tired of this.' And he shot Jeffrey right through the heart. The shocked expression on the faces of Cody and Jeffrey was enough to make his day. He aimed for the deputy, but the lawman was already on the move. Instead, Lionel raced for the wagon. He needed to grab as much gold as he could carry before whoever won the battle came to lay claim to the wagon. And if the lawman interfered, the gambler was confident he could outdraw him.

Cody used his last two bullets to put down the two injured horses. He picked up Jeffrey's discarded sidearm. It was an Adams revolver, imported from England. Cody had never seen the make before. He took no time to admire it as Lionel was headed back to the gold. He shoved the Adams into his holster and dropped the now empty Dragoon. The lawman was seething in anger at the callous way the gambler had killed Jeffrey. Opposed as he was to Jeffrey's beliefs and methods, the man had been unarmed, and had a right to surrender for trial. Now Lionel's true stripes were showing again. It would be poetic justice to take him

149

down with Jeffrey's own gun.

He got to the wagon to see the gambler was busy unloading it. 'I changed my mind. I'm not going to take all the gold. The dang wagon is too slow. I'm taking my share, though, and don't try to stop me,' said Lionel as Cody approached him, stopping thirty paces away.

'You shot an unarmed man.'

'He was going for his gun.'

'That's bull, I was right next to him. Now, you've gotta pay.'

'Spare me your sentimentality. Jeffrey was a ruthless killer. He would have done for you just as easily as I did him. I may have saved your life, you ungrateful wretch.'

Cody, taken aback by Lionel's jarring response, stiffened his spine. 'Doesn't matter, you still ain't leaving with that gold.'

Lionel dropped the bag of gold he was holding and turned around, slowly, his eyes dangerous.

'So, deputy, you want to try me? The coward of the army, making your stand? Such a long way you've come.' His tone was mocking, unfriendly. 'Make your play.'

In the distance Cody heard the rumbling of horses' hoofs; the din of battle was fading, and the victors would come to claim their spoils. His eyes straight ahead, boring a hole in Lionel, while his hand edged toward the Adams. The gambler saw the move and reached for his Navy Remington. It was now or never. Lionel had the look of a draw fighter, fast as hell. But Hank's words came back to Cody: you have reflexes of blinding speed. He let instinct take over and dragged iron.

Lionel was quicker on the draw, but Cody anticipated him and ducked low. The shot was over his head. By the time the Missourian drew a bead on Cody, the barrel of the Adams erupted in smoke. The bullet shot true, hitting Lionel square in the chest. The gambler dropped his Remington and clutched at his chest.

'Well, don't that beat all,' he gasped, then collapsed. His death rattle shuddered his body, then he was still.

Cody let out a deep breath and dropped the revolver. His hands were still shaking. This was the hardest kill, not only because Lionel was a gunman, but also because he had saved Cody's life. He had his own reasons for doing so, but if he hadn't intervened Cody could well be dead. The deputy moved to replace the gold bags Lionel had taken out, when riders approached. Looking up, he saw they wore the rebel gray, and the deputy reached for a weapon – only to realize he was unarmed.

CHAPTER 22

A bedraggled group of Confederates, led by Colonel Julius Tucker, rode up to the Conestoga. Cody counted seven of them, including the colonel. He grabbed the Adams from where the revolver had dropped, holstered it, and waited.

Julius and his men reined up. 'Corporal Livingstone, secure the wagon. Get it moving to the fort. Those Union troops could break out at any moment.' The man named Livingstone saluted and took his men to gather up the gold.

'You, I might have known.' The colonel looked beyond Cody to the dead Lionel. 'You're doing?'

Cody nodded.

'Where's Jeffrey?'

'Dead, unfortunately Colonel. Killed by Lionel Hewitt, the gambler.'

The colonel's face changed, the hard lines grew softer and he looked about to weep. Then catching himself, he took off his hat. 'Jeffrey was a good man, an excellent soldier, and a boon companion. He deserved better than to be laid low by this dreadful vermin.' His steely gray eyes bore into Cody. 'It looks like I owe you a favor, killing that scum and avenging Jeffrey's death. I'll make yours short and merciful.' He tapped the saber on his belt. 'One flick of the wrist and I will cleave your head from your shoulders. You might not even feel any pain.' He drew the sword from its scabbard and dug his spurs into his black stallion.

Cody quick drew and fired, but the stallion was too close. It reared and took the shot full on. The horse collapsed and down went Julius with a curse. The colonel untangled himself and with one swift motion brought his sword on the animal's neck, nearly cleaving it in two. Cody stared agape as the stallion thrashed in its death throes.

'You shot my best horse out from under me. Perhaps you won't die so fast after all.'

Livingstone and the other soldiers ignored the wagon and began to approach Cody, drawing their weapons. Julius put up his hand. 'Stay back, he's mine. Better yet, give him your saber, Livingstone. Shall we duel, deputy, with true warriors' weapons?'

Livingstone unbuckled his sword and tossed it at Cody's feet. Julius grinned at him manically. For a split second Cody was tempted to gun him down. But he knew he would never survive the hail of bullets that would surely come from his men. 'All right, I'll play.' He dropped Jeffrey's revolver and picked up the sword. No sooner than he unsheathed it than Julius raised his sword in salute and attacked.

Cody had no skill with the saber, he had never been

an officer or in the cavalry. He even hated to use the bayonet. His lack of skill was immediately obvious as Julius bore down on him. The colonel was deft, weaving and bobbing, cutting and slashing. Cody could barely keep his sword up as little cuts formed on his arms, and he quickly realized that Julius was toying with him. The colonel gave a deep laugh – his eyes were fiery orbs as he pushed the lawman back. The man's insane, thought Cody. He retreated from the forceful attack, disengaging and running, trying to make space between them. That only made Julius laugh all the more.

'Coward, come and face your doom.' Julius launched himself after Cody, who was bleeding from the little cuts the colonel's saber had made. Cody went wide around the wagon, ignoring the jeering from the lustful soldiers, trying to buy time. He wondered why Julius was here, if he had defeated the Union soldiers.

He didn't stand much chance against this master swordsman, and his arms were throbbing with pain. He ducked under the wagon.

'Hiding now, tsk, tsk, bad form, lawman, bad form.' Julius bent down and poked his head underneath the wagon, but got a face full of dirt. Cody kicked out, and the colonel was forced backward, bellowing in rage. Cody scrambled out and charged the Confederate, who was still rubbing his eyes. Julius barely got his sword up in time, and swore 'Dirty trickster!'

'Sort of like fighting against a man who doesn't know how to use his weapon of choice?' Cody kept the pressure on, forcing the Confederate to step back. He disengaged and brought his sword low, trying to cut out the colonel's legs. Julius jumped back, stumbled and fell. Cody was on him like a hungry wolf, wedging his sword to the ground. The colonel released his grip and Cody kicked the man in the face for good measure. It was then he heard the hammers being pulled back.

'I will allow no harm to come to the colonel. You will drop your sword and surrender,' said Livingstone.

Cody, his back still turned to Livingstone, dropped his sword. But in one move he reached down and jerked Julius to his feet, spinning him around, putting him in a choke hold. 'You shoot now, and your beloved colonel will die.' The rush of battle was wearing off and the pain in his arm muscles returned in full force. He could feel his grip loosening. He couldn't keep the bluff going for much longer. And in the end it wasn't necessary, as a bugle sounded another charge call.

Livingstone and his five men turned, just in time to see a full troop of mounted Union soldiers coming for them. Only two got their rifles to their shoulders before all of them were gunned down. Cody watched the beautiful spectacle, the tears welling up in his eyes. But in that moment, distracted, he let his guard down and Julius took advantage of it. He elbowed Cody hard in the ribs, and the lawman released his grip and fell, scrambling to find a weapon.

'I'll take you down, you son of a mangy cur!' Julius had grabbed his revolver and was readying it, when Cody's hands grasped the holstered Adams. Fitting, he thought, as he drew the Confederate officer's weapon. Still on his knees, he sent three shots into the chest of

Colonel Julius Tucker. The Confederate, his unused weapon slipping from his grasp, gave Cody a surprised look, then toppled over, dead. Cody inhaled deeply and collapsed in the dirt, sobbing with relief.

Cody woke up to find his wounded arms were bandaged, and his left arm in a sling. He was lying on a cot in an army tent, unarmed. Curious, he got up and walked outside. There he saw a familiar face sitting by a campfire, drinking coffee.

'A sight for sore eyes, if there ever was one. Howdy Hank.'

Hank Grimes turned around and smiled. 'Deputy Cody, looks like you pulled through. The doc was worried you had lost too much blood.'

'Nah, just some cuts and scratches. I think I passed out on account of exhaustion.'

'Well, whatever it was, I'm glad to see you alive.'

'So you did it, you managed to get the army here. I was worried, 'cause our good buddy Lionel Hewitt said he sent some shady characters on your back trail.'

'Yeah, them. I took care of 'em,' Hank stood up, holding a cane in one hand. 'For my leg, doc says it will get better soon. But actually I wasn't. . . .'

'He wasn't the one to bring the Union, deputy, it was me.'

Cody groaned as the new speaker came into view. 'I thought I told you to drop your pursuit and head home, Mr Talbott.'

Talbott snorted in disdain. 'Do you think I would listen to an upstart like you? Besides, I wasn't about to up and leave my gold. After our encounter most of my men had no more stomach for battle. So I headed to the nearest fort just as you said you sent Mr Grimes here. I arrived just after he did, and it was my testimony as an upstanding citizen of the Union that convinced the colonel to march.'

'I had a bit of a time convincing them, but Talbott was known to the colonel, so he trusted his word.'

'How did you find the convoy?' Cody said.

'We didn't know exactly where they were, but Colonel Smuthers thought it wise to get as close to the fort as possible and try and cut them off. They must have been delayed because we were looking for them for about a day,' said Hank.

'However you did it I am eternally grateful.'

'Not as thankful as I am to see my gold returned. Thanks to the army, that is, and not to you, deputy,' said Talbott, with a sneer. Cody was about to respond when a shout of 'Atten-Hut!' came, and the soldier began to stand to attention. Cody's stomach churned and his face filled with dread as the aforementioned Union Army Colonel Smuthers approached them. He was dressed in an impeccable blue uniform, his boots gave off a shine, his mustache was perfectly groomed. The colonel was flanked by several other men, junior officers by their insignia, and armed troopers. He stopped right in front of Cody, and eyeballed him up and down. After a long while he said, 'So you are the one who tracked these men down.'

'Yes sir, I am. Name's Cody Black, deputy sheriff of Gold Hill, and. . . .'

The colonel's eyebrows raised.

'. . . and deserter of the Union Army, 58th Ohio Infantry, sir. I deserted in the face of battle. I hereby surrender to you as an officer of the US Army for trial and punishment for my crime.'

Smuthers stepped for back a moment as if to apprise the situation. He then withdrew and stood in discussion with his officers out of earshot for a long time. Then he came and stood right in front of Cody. 'What you say is the truth?'

Cody nodded, his throat dry.

'And you killed Colonel Julius Tucker?'

Again, Cody nodded.

'And his second, Major Jeffrey Cranster?'

'No,' Cody croaked, 'that was someone else, but I ended up killing him, too.'

'A Union man?'

'No, a gambler who went in with the Confederates, then betrayed them, and me.'

'Ah, after the gold I see.'

Cody nodded at the remark. Smuthers conferred with his men again, then apparently reached a decision, and approached Cody.

'What was your rank?'

'Private.'

'Private Cody Black of the 58th Ohio Infantry, in the light of these revelations, and indeed in the light of your exceptional valor in the face of overwhelming odds and helping to defeat an enemy of the state, I declare your secret mission, wherein you pretend to desert from the army and disguise yourself as a civilian lawman in order to ferret out this most treasonous of plots, a success.'

Cody blinked, and looked at the colonel in stunned surprise. The Union officer spoke with a clipped cadence so he wasn't sure he had heard him correctly. Before he could speak Smuthers held up his hand. 'I will inform your commander in the 17th by courier that your mission was successful, and you will remain attached to my command, at the rank of corporal, for the remainder of the war.'

'Sir, thank you sir. I, but my. . . .' he touched the star on his chest.

'Ah yes, your duties as sheriff of Gold Hill will be taken over by a suitable replacement.' He looked meaningfully at Hank.

Hank scratched his head and smiled. 'Sure, I can keep the chair warm for you, until you return, that is.'

Cody punched his arm lightly. 'You do that. After the war, I'll come up and visit.'

Talbott looked on, exasperated by what he was witnessing. 'But he was just a coward who . . . oh, never mind. What about my gold?'

Smuthers turned his attention to the mining baron. 'Your gold, in fact all of this gold, was confiscated by Confederate forces and ultimately recovered by federal troops. Therefore it will remain the property of the US Army until the war's over. We will transfer the gold to Denver, and hold it on an army post there for safe keeping.'

Talbott looked dazed, the color in his cheeks gone. 'End of the war! But how long is that? Colonel, please,

I beseech you.' Smuthers waved his hand in dismissal and left, Talbott trailing him, still begging.

'Looks like Talbott got about what he deserved,' said Hank, who seemed unperturbed at losing his own gold. Chortling, Hank continued, 'At least I'm set up with a plum job. What are you gonna do now?'

The newly installed corporal still couldn't get over his shock at being pardoned by the colonel. Cody the coward had returned as Cody the soldier. 'Now, I need a bath and about two pints of whiskey. But I'll settle for some grub first.' Hank laughed, and clapped his friend on the back as the two walked toward the nearby chuck wagon.